Dear Reader,

We're thrilled that some of Harlequin's most famous families are making an encore appearance! With this special Famous Families fifty-book collection, we are proud to offer you the chance to relive the drama, the glamour, the suspense and the romance of four of Harlequin's most beloved families—the Fortunes, the Bravos, the McCabes and the Cavanaughs.

Our third family, the McCabes, welcomes you to Laramie, Texas. A small ranching town of brick buildings, awnings and shady streets, Laramie is the kind of place where everyone knows each other. The little town is currently abuzz with wedding plans—and no McCabe is safe from the matchmaking! The path to the altar may not be smooth for the McCabes, but their humor-filled journeys will no doubt bring a smile to your face.

And in August, you'll be captivated by our final family, the Cavanaughs. Generations of Cavanaughs have protected the citizens of Aurora, California. But can they protect themselves from falling in love? You won't want to miss any of these stories from *USA TODAY* bestselling author Marie Ferrarella!

Happy reading,

The Editors

CATHY GILLEN THACKER

is married and a mother of three. She and her husband spent eighteen years in Texas and now reside in North Carolina. Her mysteries, romantic comedies and heartwarming family stories have made numerous appearances on bestseller lists, but her best reward, she says, is knowing one of her books made someone's day a little brighter.

A popular Harlequin Books author for many years, she loves telling passionate stories with happy endings, and thinks nothing beats a good romance and a hot cup of tea! You can visit Cathy's website at www.cathygillenthacker.com for more information on her upcoming and previously published books, recipes and a list of her favorite things.

FAMOUS FAMILIES
the McCABES

CATHY GILLEN THACKER

Wildcat Cowboy

™ **Harlequin**®

TORONTO NEW YORK LONDON
AMSTERDAM PARIS SYDNEY HAMBURG
STOCKHOLM ATHENS TOKYO MILAN MADRID
PRAGUE WARSAW BUDAPEST AUCKLAND

Recycling programs
for this product may
not exist in your area.

ISBN-13: 978-0-373-36505-0

WILDCAT COWBOY

Copyright © 1999 by Cathy Gillen Thacker

All rights reserved. Except for use in any review, the reproduction or utilization of this work in whole or in part in any form by any electronic, mechanical or other means, now known or hereafter invented, including xerography, photocopying and recording, or in any information storage or retrieval system, is forbidden without the written permission of the publisher, Harlequin Enterprises Limited, 225 Duncan Mill Road, Don Mills, Ontario M3B 3K9, Canada.

This is a work of fiction. Names, characters, places and incidents are either the product of the author's imagination or are used fictitiously, and any resemblance to actual persons, living or dead, business establishments, events or locales is entirely coincidental.

This edition published by arrangement with Harlequin Books S.A.

For questions and comments about the quality of this book please contact us at Customer_eCare@Harlequin.ca.

® and TM are trademarks of the publisher. Trademarks indicated with ® are registered in the United States Patent and Trademark Office, the Canadian Trade Marks Office and in other countries.

www.Harlequin.com

Printed in U.S.A.

FAMOUS FAMILIES

The Fortunes

Cowboy at Midnight by Ann Major
A Baby Changes Everything by Marie Ferrarella
In the Arms of the Law by Peggy Moreland
Lone Star Rancher by Laurie Paige
The Good Doctor by Karen Rose Smith
The Debutante by Elizabeth Bevarly
Keeping Her Safe by Myrna Mackenzie
The Law of Attraction by Kristi Gold
Once a Rebel by Sheri WhiteFeather
Military Man by Marie Ferrarella
Fortune's Legacy by Maureen Child
The Reckoning by Christie Ridgway

The Bravos by Christine Rimmer

The Nine-Month Marriage
Marriage by Necessity
Practically Married
Married by Accident
The Millionaire She Married
The M.D. She Had to Marry
The Marriage Agreement
The Bravo Billionaire
The Marriage Conspiracy
His Executive Sweetheart
Mercury Rising
Scrooge and the Single Girl

Chapter 1

The moment the black-and-gray helicopter swooped into sight and landed behind the Golden Slipper ranch house, a half mile down the road, Josie Wyatt knew that trouble was on the way. And sure enough it arrived on her doorstep in the form of Houston multimillionaire Wade McCabe several minutes later.

He drove up in a black Ford Expedition truck and parked adjacent to the four Wyatt Drilling Company trailers and the towering, twenty-eight-foot rig. Her heart pounding, Josie watched as the ruggedly fit, six-foot-plus businessman-investor climbed down from the truck and started across the gravel parking area. For a moment he simply stood there in the hot Texas sun, hands braced on his hips, staring in mute disapproval at the ancient rotary-drill oil rig. Josie heard him mutter several choice words before he swung around and strode toward her in a grim-faced, take-charge, all-male way that made her throat go dry.

He was wearing black jeans, a pale sage-green silk-linen shirt and darker sage-green tie. A creased black Stetson was pulled low across his brow. Sexy aviator sunglasses shaded his eyes. High, flat cheekbones framed a blade-straight nose, and the masculine set and shape of his jaw indicated this was not a Texan to be messed with.

His sensually chiseled lips curving slightly upward, he clasped her hand in his. "Wade McCabe. I'm looking for Big Jim Wyatt."

Josie had been afraid of that. And unfortunately, she thought, as tingles of sexual awareness swept all the way up her arm, since she was momentarily the only one on the drilling site, it was left to her to deliver the bad news. Giving him a welcoming smile, Josie extricated her much smaller hand from his.

"Big Jim is in South America," she replied, keeping her eyes on his.

This was *not* what Wade McCabe wanted to hear, Josie knew.

"And he didn't even call me to let me know he was leaving the country?" Wade demanded irately as he whipped off his sunglasses and tucked them in the pocket of his shirt.

Josie tried not to get her dander up as she stared into the most beautiful pair of dark brown eyes she had ever seen. "He left on very short notice, but there's no cause for concern. There's still a four-person team working on your site, including me."

Wade McCabe shook his head in barely suppressed

aggravation, swept off his Stetson and slapped it against his thigh. Still looking her over from head to toe, he drawled sarcastically, "And have you struck oil yet?"

Josie ignored the utter lack of confidence in Wade McCabe's tone as she squared her slender shoulders to face off with the owner of the land. "It's gonna happen any day now," she stated firmly.

"Uh-huh." His eyes still locked with hers, Wade McCabe blew out a disbelieving breath and swept a hand through the rumpled ash-brown layers of his hair. He set his hat on his head and tugged it low across his brow. "Get Big Jim on the phone," he ordered, closing in on her. "Now."

"I can't." A warm flush filled Josie's cheeks as she backed toward the trailer that was serving as their on-site office and laboratory.

"Why not?" Wade McCabe snapped, keeping pace, as Josie headed up the steps.

"Because he's in a remote jungle that's miles from any phone," Josie replied, ignoring the calmly assessing glint in his chocolate-brown eyes. She held the door, ushering them both into air-conditioned comfort. "In fact, it's impossible for me to even get a message to him until he gets to a place where he can call in again."

Wade McCabe blew out a frustrated breath as he shut the aluminum door behind them and braced his broad shoulders against the frame. "And he didn't see fit to let me know any of this, even after I'd signed and returned the drilling contract?"

Big Jim didn't know about this contract. It had come in after he'd taken the rest of his crew with him to

South America and left Josie in charge of the Midland-Odessa office.

"You know you can trust Wyatt Drilling," Josie said. In fact, in the past Big Jim had done plenty of drilling contracts with Wade McCabe and had quickly and efficiently struck oil with every discovery well he drilled for him.

"I sure as heck thought I could," Wade returned as he shoved away from the door. "Otherwise I never would have just signed the papers and sent them back with a hefty check to begin operations, without at least first talking to Big Jim."

Josie stacked the sample logs that she had been studying on her desk. "I'm sure your faith hasn't been misplaced," she said stubbornly.

Finished, she folded her arms in front of her.

"I might believe that, if a modern jackknife derrick were sitting on my property," he replied, raising his voice. "Which brings me to my next point. Where in blue blazes did y'all get that hunk of metal out there?"

Josie glanced out the window at the drill that was—even now—grinding away, rhythmically digging into the earth. The steel A-frame structure looked much like a radio tower and was topped off by a crown block that was threaded with long steel cables that held the traveling block to which the hook, swivel and drill were all attached. Two sets of metal stairs ran up the sides of the derrick to the metal platform that served as the derrick floor. On that were two small shed-size buildings. One was the toolhouse. The other contained the powerful engines that ran the rig. At ground level were the slush pit and mud pump. None of it was pretty, shiny or new, but it was doing its job, and for a fraction of the cost of a new rig. As far as Josie was concerned, that was all that counted.

"That hunk of metal—as you so unkindly put it— came from Big Jim's warehouse," she said as she held Wade McCabe's steady, probing gaze. "And, I'll have you know, it has quite a history."

Wade rubbed his jaw with the flat of his hand and glanced out the window at the grunting, groaning machinery. "I'll bet."

"Big Jim found his very first producing well with that rig." Josie was hoping—for reasons that were both practical and sentimental—that it would also help *her* strike oil for the first time. "Furthermore," she added, "you should be pleased to know that this particular rig is costing you only one-tenth of the expense of the rig we've used in the past on your various leases." That ought to appeal to a man who spent all his time making money.

He squinted at her, taking his time about it, before he returned his insultingly frank gaze to her face. "What'd you say your name was again?"

She hadn't, Josie thought, swearing inwardly. But she would have to now. "Josie. Josie Lynn Corbett," Josie replied reluctantly, deliberately leaving out the last part of her hyphenated last name, which was way too long, anyway, thanks to her parents, who'd never been able to agree on anything even before she was born.

"Well, Josie," Wade McCabe drawled, "you tell Big Jim I've never been one to drill down a dry hole for long. Never mind with substandard equipment and a second-string crew! And that being the case, I'm pulling out now."

Josie's mouth fell open. "Wait a minute," she protested hotly as she circled around her desk and grabbed him by the arm. "You can't do that!"

Wade looked askance at the feminine hand curved around his bicep. "Watch me!"

Josie moved to block his way, putting herself between Wade and the door. "Quitting now would be like throwing all this hard work we've done away!"

"And speaking of that, exactly what part do you play in this?" Wade demanded.

Josie stepped past the dual phones, computer, printer, fax and copier and plucked the drilling and billing records for the site from her desk, which she promptly handed over. "I'm acting site coordinator, and I'm also handling the financial end of things plus all the record keeping and necessary paperwork."

Wade carefully perused the drilling and billing records she'd handed over. Apparently unable to find anything amiss, he finally looked up. His glance swept her from head to toe, taking in every inch of her snug-fitting blue jeans, electric blue T-shirt and dusty red cowboy boots before returning with slow deliberation to her face. "I've never known Big Jim to employ any women."

As his gaze settled on the delicate features of her oval face, Josie did her best to suppress a moue of regret. "Unfortunately, in the past that's been true."

"Then why did he hire you?" Wade persisted as their eyes clashed and held.

Feeling her abilities were in question, Josie lifted her

chin defiantly. "Because I'm an aspiring land woman myself." She wanted to be able to find the land, acquire the mineral leases and put the deals together. And then make it all work. "And I told him I wanted to learn all about the oil business from the ground up from the very best locator of wildcat wells in Texas. I'm persistent as all get-out when I want something, and I talked him into it."

Seeing the start of an appreciative grin on Wade's face, Josie settled on the edge of her desk and continued more easily, "And, to be perfectly blunt, with Big Jim and most of his regular crew in South America on that emergency, they needed some additional hands-on help on this project for Gus, our resident equipment expert, Dieter, our geophysicist, and Ernie, our petroleum engineer." Overall, the experience for her had been invaluable.

"Couldn't they have hired another roughneck for that?"

"I'm perfectly competent to help out the guys in any number of ways, I assure you." In fact, she was more than competent. And furthermore, Big Jim would have seen that firsthand when she'd started working for him six months ago, Josie thought irately, *if* he'd just taken into account her wide range of experience and given her half a chance, instead of relegating her to answering phones and doing silly errands and filing papers for him.

"Yeah, well," Wade McCabe continued to glance at Josie skeptically, "be that as it may, I'm still pulling out."

Was the trailer smaller with him in it or was that her

imagination? "Now wait just a minute," Josie countered, irked to find McCabe every bit as chauvinistic in his attitude toward her as her very own father. "Wyatt Drilling has always struck oil for you in the past, haven't they?"

Wade McCabe nodded. "Which is why I hired Big Jim Wyatt and not someone else to do the drilling. 'Cause I didn't want to pour thousands of dollars down some dry hole in a vain search for black gold where none was to be found."

"There is oil on this property," Josie announced adamantly.

"I don't doubt that for a moment," Wade agreed complacently. "Otherwise I never would have bought the property for myself and acquired the lease. But if you and Big Jim and the rest of his outfit think I'm gonna just empty my pockets while Big Jim's second-string stand-ins fumble around finding it for me, while he and the rest of his regular top-notch crew are off in South America, working for somebody else, you are sadly mistaken. So you can tell Big Jim if and when he calls—" Wade took the contract signed with Big Jim's scrawled initials, JLW, and his own name out of his back pocket, and tore it in two. "That I'm invoking the quit clause, and the deal is off. Now."

As Wade pressed the ripped-up contract into her hands and curled her resisting fingers around it, perspiration beaded Josie's pretty brow. Color swept into her high, delicately sculpted cheeks. Desperation colored her vibrant azure-blue eyes. "Please. Don't do this," she said.

"Believe me," Wade retorted gruffly, knowing this woman was a distraction he did not need, "I'd rather not have been put in this position, either. I've trusted your boss for a long time, Josie Corbett. To find out he's let me down—" Wade's throat tightened. He was so disappointed in Big Jim and Wyatt Drilling he found he couldn't go on. Betrayal—on any level—was something he did not tolerate easily these days.

She reached around behind her and put the contract right next to a big roll of scotch tape. Turning around, she focused her guileless eyes on his. "Wyatt Drilling's never failed to give you a producing well yet," she said again in desperation.

Wade shrugged haplessly and stuck his thumbs through the belt loops on either side of his fly. "He might not have now, either, had he been the one here, supervising."

Silence fell between them. Unable to bear the raw disappointment in her eyes, or the knowledge that he had put it there, Wade let his glance fall to the stack of partially opened mail on Josie's desk. One large envelope in particular caught his eye. Spilling out of it were dozens of pictures of pretty dresses that had been torn out of magazines.

"Big date coming up?" Wade prodded dryly, wondering why even the thought of Josie out on the town with someone else did not go down well with him.

Josie shoved her hands in the back of her form-fitting blue jeans and scowled. "Don't be ridiculous," she said, glaring at him as if she wouldn't be caught dead in anything feminine or glamorous. "If you're thinking I tore those pages out of magazines, think again!"

Without the proof, Wade wouldn't have suspected Josie of harboring any Cinderella dreams. As stunningly attractive as she was, she looked like a tomboy through and through. Her glossy dark brown hair had been caught in a bouncy ponytail at the back of her head. Silken tendrils escaped to drape her slender neck and frame her pretty oval face. She didn't appear to be wearing any makeup on the delicate features of her face—not that her flawless golden skin, high model's cheekbones, thickly lashed eyes and softly luscious lips would have needed much in any case.

Obviously guessing at the direction of his thoughts, Josie's lower lip slid out truculently, and her eyes turned an even stormier blue. "Those pictures were sent to me by my mother."

Wade wasn't sure how he felt about the effort to get Josie into an incredibly gorgeous evening gown or not.

It would be exciting as all get-out to see her in a dress that was cut up to here and down to there and showed a good deal of décolletage as well as an expanse of long, lissome thigh. But on the other hand her snug-fitting T-shirt molded her breasts as softly and precisely as a lover's caress. Her slim-fitting jeans similarly outlined her slender waist, just-right hips and long, sexy legs.

More to the point, Wade conceded appreciatively to himself, Josie's jeans, T-shirt and dusty red western boots were more suited to the briskly energetic, sexily purposeful way she moved. Here, at last, was a woman who could hold her own in any situation, no matter how challenging or physical. Any situation except—Wade noted, while Josie did her best to swiftly gather up the pictures and shove them in a drawer, out of view—perhaps this.

"So your mother wants to see you all gussied up?" Wade guessed.

Josie shrugged and assumed an aura of supreme boredom. "She and my father both want me married off."

"Then they probably don't want you working out here, do they?"

"Given their druthers, no, they wouldn't." Josie sighed and, looking relieved to be able to talk about something else beside Wade's crushing disappointment in Big Jim, continued in a low, disappointed tone, "Both of them hope that by working for Wyatt Drilling I'll get this dream of mine, of being a wildcatter, out of my system once and for all. In the meantime," Josie's voluptuous lips thinned, "my mother is trying every way possible to let me know I'll never find the perfect man unless I live in the city and look like those magazine pictures all the time!"

"She may have a point, you know." Wade grinned and decided to throw in his two cents. "I know I prefer women in satin and silk." In fact, for a variety of reasons, women like that were the only kind he dated.

"Well, that's not me," Josie said flatly.

He studied the new flood of color in her cheeks. Unable to resist teasing her, he said, "I can see where it'd be a stretch." Although she clearly had the figure to wear anything she wanted, Wade couldn't really see the Texas tomboy wearing any of the sexy dresses in those magazine ads.

Josie gave him a measuring look. "You're telling me

I don't look like some Dallas debutante?" she asked sweetly.

If the Dallas debs looked anything like the Houston debs where he was currently living? "I'd have to say no," Wade replied reluctantly. None of them would have been caught dead living out in the middle of the Texas countryside, working an oil rig.

Josie draped a hand across her breasts and breathed a sigh of what appeared to be heartfelt relief. "Good."

He quirked a brow.

"It was never my ambition to wear pretty dresses like a model or be a deb, anyway," Josie told him frankly.

Wade wasn't so sure about that—didn't all little girls pine for stuff like that when they were growing up?— but for the sake of her feelings he let her remark pass undisputed. Resisting the urge to smooth a strand of silky brown hair from her cheek, he soothed her as best he could, "I imagine you're a little old for all that debutante stuff, anyway." No use in her crying for what she couldn't have. No use in him pining after what he shouldn't have!

"I'm twenty-six. Not—" Josie tossed her head "—that it's any of your business."

"Well, I'm thirty." Wade's lips curved wryly. "Not that it's any of your business." He frowned as the cell phone in his pocket began to ring. "Mind if I take this in here?"

"Be my guest." Josie quickly finished straightening her desk while he answered his call. To his chagrin, the news was not good.

"Problem?" Josie said when he'd hung up.

Wade nodded, grimacing. "My events planner just

quit on me. Which is what I get, I suppose, for hiring someone I once dated."

"Why'd she take the job if she found it uncomfortable working for you?"

"To teach me a lesson, apparently." Despite his ex-girlfriend's anger, Wade had no regrets about ending their relationship. He knew in the final analysis they had been all wrong for each other. His inability to confide in her, the loneliness he'd felt when he was with her, had been proof of that. "Andrea wanted me to know what it feels like to be left high and dry. Especially since—if what she said just now is to be believed—it's now way too late to get anyone good to come all the way out to Laramie to handle the party for me."

Wade frowned as he slid his wallet-size cell phone in the back pocket of his jeans. "Of course, given Andrea's background, I probably should have seen this coming. And known better than to deal with someone who was so emotional and reckless with money."

Josie quirked a brow. "What do you mean?"

"Andrea's a former deb. She's got a healthy trust fund. She doesn't need the money from her business to live on. She just uses it to give her some sort of identity, aside from her family's wealth and social standing."

Josie flushed. Looking distinctly uncomfortable with the subject, she turned away from him and paced restlessly. "When is this party of yours?"

Glad to be able to talk about something besides his ex-girlfriend, Wade stepped close enough to be able to look into Josie's face and inhale the surprisingly warm and sensual orange blossom perfume. "Friday night."

Josie's pretty eyes widened. "This Friday? Five days from now?"

Wade nodded.

Josie clucked her tongue against the roof of her mouth. She shook her head at him, regarding him sympathetically. "Then Andrea's probably right."

Wade looked at her curiously.

"It's June—which is prime wedding season," Josie explained patiently. "Every reliable party planner in the state has probably already been booked for months now."

Wade shrugged. "I'll just take care of the party myself, then."

Josie considered that a moment. "That might be possible. What kind of party is it?"

"My parents are both retiring from Laramie Community Hospital in the next few weeks, and I thought I'd give them a proper send-off."

Josie picked up a notepad and pen and dropped into the swivel chair behind her desk, propping her boot-clad feet on the edge. "You've at least rented a space to hold the party, I hope?"

Wade nodded as he tore his eyes from her long legs. "The Laramie Community Center. That's one detail I took care of myself."

She scribbled that down and put a check beside it. "Do you have a contract with a caterer?" He shook his head, aware from the look on her face that was a major faux pas.

"Theme?" Josie prodded, scribbling some more.

Again he shook his head. And was rewarded with another lightning round of questions.

"Decorations? Band? DJ? Flowers or centerpieces?" she pressed.

"None of the above," Wade admitted reluctantly as he perched on the edge of her battered wooden desk. "But I'll handle it. I can do anything I set my mind to."

Josie made a few more notes on the pad in front of her. "I suppose that means you'll be staying in town, then."

"I'm gonna have to," Wade said.

"Good, then." She looked up at him. "Because—"

Wade put up a silencing hand. "It's not going to change my mind about the drilling, though. I still want to pull the plug."

Josie cupped her chin between her forefinger and thumb. Looking more determined than ever to come out the winner in this, she regarded him thoughtfully. "What if I could get Wyatt Drilling to share the risk and absorb the costs of the drilling from this point forward, in exchange for a 2 percent higher royalty rate over the life of the well, if we do strike oil? Would you let us continue then?"

Chapter 2

To Josie's immediate intense relief, Wade McCabe looked tempted by her offer. Very tempted. "How are you going to do that with Big Jim out of the country?" he demanded. He picked up a pencil and turned it end over end.

"Big Jim made provisions with his bank and his attorneys for any contingency that might come up when he was in South America. I'll talk to both parties promptly," Josie continued in a soft, coaxing voice, drawing on every ounce of persuasiveness she possessed.

"They know how it is in the oil business. Sometimes unusual financial arrangements have to be made in order to continue exploration, but it all works out in the end." Josie paused and bit her lip. "The bottom line is that Big Jim has always been reasonable. And, with

Wyatt Drilling's reputation at stake here…well, you know how much your business in the past has meant to Big Jim. And how much we all hope it will mean in the future. So it only makes sense that we do whatever necessary to help you—us—continue with the drilling," Josie said as the trailer door slammed and a grizzled old roughneck she loved almost as much as her own father strode in.

At five foot five, he was shorter than Josie by several inches, his stocky frame muscled from head to toe. He wore a red-plaid long-sleeved shirt, buttoned at the neck, jeans and thick leather construction boots. His deeply suntanned face sported several days growth of beard, and the pewter gray hair sticking out from beneath his banged-up, yellow hard hat was buzz-cut close to his head with one of those home barber kits in a no-nonsense style that mirrored his personality.

There was never any telling what Gus might say, if the spirit moved him; he had a habit of speaking his mind.

Josie turned to Gus. "Isn't that right, Gus?" she said meaningfully, giving him a look that let him know the situation was precarious, and warned him to watch what he said around Wade McCabe. "Big Jim would want Mr. McCabe to be satisfied with the work Wyatt Drilling is doing for him on his land."

"I know it for a fact," Gus said. Wiping the grease from his hands with a rag, he looked at Josie, then Wade. "I feel as sure as Josie here that we're very, very close to striking oil. Otherwise, I'd shut the operation down myself in a heartbeat. You have my word on that, McCabe."

Wade sighed. He didn't know how or why he was letting himself be talked into this. He'd come here sure of what he wanted to do if he didn't talk to Big Jim face-to-face. But between Josie's soft pleading looks and Gus's man-to-man assurance, he could feel himself folding, and that was curious. It wasn't like him to be a soft touch, especially when it came to business. And especially when he still had this nagging feeling that Josie wasn't telling him everything.

"I suppose if you'll guarantee Wyatt Drilling will absorb the cost of the drilling from this day forward until we strike," he conceded reluctantly at last, knowing Gus—at least—had worked on other discovery wells for Wade that had ultimately become producers.

Josie stepped forward hurriedly. "We'll get permission and have papers drawn up for you to sign ASAP," she promised.

"Or else shut it down pronto," Gus added. "Again at no further charge to you."

"Okay." Wade capitulated, appreciating the excited sparkle in Josie's eyes. He stood very still and studied both their faces. "I'll do it, but only for a 1 percent royalty rate increase over the life of the well, not 2," he stipulated determinedly. "Agreed?"

Josie and Gus exchanged tenuous looks, then finally nodded. "Agreed," Josie and Gus said as the three of them shook hands all around.

"I'm headed over to the hospital in Laramie to see my brother Jackson. You can find me there or at my parents' ranch." Wade McCabe scrawled down both addresses and phone numbers on a piece of paper and handed them to Josie, his fingers brushing against her softer ones in the process. "Whatever happens, I want to know as soon as it's decided," he warned firmly. He wondered if the rest of her skin was as smooth and soft.

Looking incredibly relieved, Josie nodded. She moved her hand away from his. "Gus or I will get back to you personally," she promised.

"Have you lost your mind?" Gus said as soon as Wade McCabe's truck had disappeared from view and he'd heard the rest of her plans. "Dipping into your own trust fund to pay for drilling on someone else's property?"

"What choice did I have?" Josie replied, knowing she was already personally subsidizing the rest of the costs on this project that were not being directly billed to Wade McCabe. "If I hadn't offered to absorb the costs he would have shut us down on the spot!"

Josie went to the refrigerator and brought out the pitcher of iced tea. Finding it almost empty, she set about brewing some more.

"Considering the way things have been going, maybe we should shut down until your father gets back from South America," Gus continued as Josie got out two quart-size tea bags and put them in the top of the tea maker.

"Not you, too!" Josie filled the bottom with cold water from the tap.

Gus watched her put the tea maker together, plug it in and turn it on with a flick of the switch. "I know you have the talent for scenting out oil, Josie," he said gently. Taking a paper towel from the round wooden holder, he dampened it with cold water and mopped his leathery, bewhiskered face. "Your father and I have both known it since you were a kid." Gus paused, still holding the towel to the back of his sunburned neck. "But your father would skin me alive if he knew what you were doing, girl, and you know it."

Josie folded her arms in front of her and regarded Gus stubbornly. "He told me to take care of things on this end."

"Knowing darn well there was nothing here for you to do, since he'd leased out all the rest of his equipment, except that one old rig, which we both know he keeps mainly for sentimental reasons."

Her dad's old rig held sentimental value for her, too; that was the rig he'd used when he went from employee—on someone else's rig—to being an independent oilman. Josie had been five. She'd been visiting him at the site when he'd struck oil on one of his own leases for the very first time. It had been an incredibly exciting period of their life, and the start of what was now a very successful independently owned business. It had also required a lot of risk on her dad's part and a lot of courage. The same kind of gumption and hard work Josie hoped she was demonstrating now.

"Did you tell him your last name?" Gus continued his interrogation.

Josie plucked a lemon from the refrigerator shelf and shut the door with her hip. "Just the first half of it." And about that she did feel guilty. Josie didn't like secrets of any kind. Full and open communication was the key to people understanding each other. Unfortunately her parents—who were as different as night and day—had never learned that. Consequently, they were still on different wavelengths to this very day.

"Then you're scamming him!" Gus said.

Josie sliced the lemon and placed them artistically in the dish. Making iced tea was one of the few culinary chores she could do. "If I told Wade McCabe my last name, then it wouldn't take him long to find out—or figure out—everything else about me and my background. And you know as well as I do that no one is going to hire a former debutante to dig for oil! I don't care what her lineage or last name is!"

Gus shook his head. "We're courting disaster here," he predicted gloomily.

Josie let out an exasperated sigh. She went to the refrigerator and brought out two trays of ice. "You worry too much," she scolded as she emptied cubes into the glass pitcher.

"And you, girl, don't worry enough!"

That wasn't quite true, Josie thought. She'd done nothing but worry since she started this. But at the same time she was proud of herself. Taking risks had always been hard for her. And in this particular business, you didn't get anywhere unless you were capable of taking risks. Big ones.

If all went well here, as she and Gus and Dieter and Ernie expected it eventually would, then her decision to do this additional business for Big Jim would be proved right. And maybe, just maybe she would succeed in finally getting her mother and father both to look at her in a new light and accept her as she was, rather than what they both wanted her to be. Heaven knew she was tired of all the role-playing, tired of striving to please them, of trying to be two different types of women for two very different parents. Only to feel, ultimately, that she had somehow failed and disappointed them both. "You're wrong, Gus. I know what's at stake here," Josie said gently as she brought down two glasses from the cupboard. Noting the tea had stopped brewing, she poured it over the ice in the pitcher. "If I fail, it's not just my own butt on the line here. It's Big Jim's rep, too."

"Not to mention my friendship with Big Jim that, I'm happy to remind you, goes back some thirty-five years," Gus grumbled bad temperedly.

Josie filled two glasses, added lemon slices to both and handed one to Gus. "Never mind the fact Big Jim will find out what I've done, in going behind his back. With no good news—in the form of my success—to soften the blow."

Gus stirred three teaspoons of sugar into his tea. "So why don't you quit now and 'fess up while your dad can still come in and save the day? If not today, then eventually?" Gus demanded.

Josie sipped her tea. "Because it isn't necessary, Gus." Josie believed in herself enough to put her money where her mouth was, and it was time everyone else did, too. She leaned forward earnestly. "I know I can do this. I know I can hit oil. I just need a little more time." And one way or another, Josie decided, determined, she was going to see she got it. She'd come too far, risked too much, to back out now.

"Can't get a date for Friday evening to save your life, huh?"

Scowling, Wade hung up the phone on his brother,

Jackson McCabe's, desk. Like Wade, Jackson had spent his late teens and twenties living in other parts of Texas, but now, as one of two newly appointed general surgeons at Laramie Community Hospital, he was back for good, married to the love of his life, and busy settling into the office suite where he would see his patients.

"Can you believe it?" Wade replied, frustrated beyond belief. His plan for getting another gal pal to help him plan the party Friday night and then attend it with him had failed dismally. "It's like they've all suddenly been comparing notes!"

"Imagine that," Jackson said dryly as he hung his undergraduate diploma on the wall behind his desk.

Wade closed his little black book with a snap. He was afraid he was running out of options here. He stood and began to pace. "They all say I'm too picky. Always trying to make them over." He stopped and shook his head. He really didn't understand it. "I'm only trying to help them be all they can be."

Jackson regarded him with amused eyes and a straight face. "Hard to imagine why they wouldn't cotton to that."

Wade knew where this was going, and he didn't want to hear it. He aimed a lecturing finger at Jackson and regarded him sternly. "Just because you got married to the love of your life a few days ago, and our parents are renewing their wedding vows at the end of this month, doesn't mean the rest of us McCabes should start looking to get married, too."

Jackson grinned like the satisfied new husband he was and continued measuring and marking the wall with ruler and pencil. Due to their responsibilities as physicians in the community, Jackson and Lacey's honeymoon had been delayed. But that was okay, they had both said, because every day they spent together as man and wife was a honeymoon. And Wade had to admit—Jackson had never looked better.

Jackson paused and winked at Wade salaciously. "Don't knock it until you've tried it."

Wade grimaced and handed Jackson a picture hook. "I have tried it, remember? Sandra and I couldn't even make it through the engagement."

Jackson finished hammering and hung his med school diploma on the wall, too. "That's because Sandra was all wrong for you."

Wade conceded that now, reluctantly, but he hadn't thought so at the time.

"You just haven't met the right woman yet," Jackson continued, adding his residency and board certification diplomas beside the other two. "When you do, take it from me, you'll fall like a ton of bricks."

Jackson stared out the window at Laramie's Main Street. The downtown area dated back one hundred years and was comprised of a number of impeccably maintained neat white brick buildings with colorful awnings, inscribed with the names of the various businesses, shops and offices. He had grown up here. And he loved it still.

Realizing he was feeling a little homesick, not sure why, Wade turned back to face Jackson. "Now you sound like Mom."

"She's right." Jackson gave the diploma frames a

final straightening, then looked up as a knock sounded at the door.

Manila folder in hand, Josie Lynn Corbett strode in. She was still in the same boots, jeans, T-shirt, the bandana still knotted around her neck. The only things she'd added were sunglasses and lip gloss. So why then, Wade wondered, was his pulse suddenly pounding like he'd just run a 10-k race? Why was he suddenly viewing her like a woman he'd like to date? Why couldn't he seem to take his eyes off her? She wasn't even his type! It wasn't like he was going to pull her in his arms, take down her hair and run his fingers through it and deliver a steamy kiss to those soft, sexy lips of hers! Not in this lifetime, anyway!

Josie headed straight for him. She opened the folder for his perusal and stood close enough for him to see. "As you can tell, a special bank account has been set up to fund continued drilling on your property. All you have to do is sign all three copies of it and we'll be all set." Ignoring the warmth of her bare arm pressed up against his, Wade studied the simple, straightforward language of the contract.

"Isn't anyone gonna introduce me?" Jackson asked, stepping forward.

For reasons he didn't want to examine, Wade was very glad his handsome brother was now taken. "Jackson, Josie Lynn Corbett, from out at the drilling site," he murmured without looking up. "Josie, my brother Jackson McCabe."

Josie strode forward in her loose and sexy tomboy stride. She took Jackson's hand and shook it. "Nice to meet you."

While Wade signed the contracts, Jackson continued to study Josie, long after their brief handshake ended. "Have we met?" Jackson asked finally.

Josie stiffened at the question and shook her head. Wade looked up, wondering what was going on here.

"You sure?" Jackson persisted with a lot less tact than usual. "You look awfully familiar."

"I have one of those faces. I'm always being told that I look like someone's sister or cousin." Josie laughed nervously.

Like hell she did, Wade thought. Josie Lynn Corbett was one of the most natural beauties he'd ever seen in his life. There was nothing common about her. From the top of her head to the ends of her toes she was one memorable woman. And it irked him to think that his brother Jackson-successful surgeon and former play-boy—might have somehow known her first.

"I'm sure you have me mixed up with someone else," Josie continued.

Wade hoped that was the case.

Jackson shook his head and continued to look perplexed. "I could swear—I never forget a face." He paused, stroking his jaw. "You're not from around here, I guess?"

A self-conscious flush pinkened Josie's cheeks. "No."

"Where do you hail from?" Wade asked as he handed over two of the signed contracts and kept one for himself. Generally speaking, tomboys weren't his type. But there was something about this one that caught—and held—his attention. He was even more surprised to find out how curious he was about her, her present, her past.

Josie accepted the papers Wade gave her with a businesslike nod and small smile. Looking for a moment as if the information was being dragged out of her, she said, "I grew up in the Dallas-Fort Worth area."

"Really? I was just there!" Jackson snapped his fingers. "In fact, I almost took a job in town. Maybe we met there."

Unfortunately for her, Josie thought uneasily, she and Jackson McCabe probably had encountered each other. Not randomly, but at a Corbett Foundation-sponsored gala. The foundation was always raising money for local hospitals. And if she wasn't mistaken, Jackson McCabe had been at one several months ago, as part of a large group of surgeons. But she couldn't have him remembering that! Because then he would also be likely to recall she had been sitting on the dais!

Noticing Wade was watching her even more closely than his brother, Josie shrugged and turned her glance back to Jackson. "Maybe you saw me around Laramie pumping gas or buying groceries," she suggested lightly, wishing Wade would quit watching her with such interest.

Jackson shook his head and continued to look baffled. "I don't think that's it."

Before Josie could back her way out of the door, a sixty-something woman in a pink sweater and a white nurse's uniform waltzed in. Her name tag said Lilah McCabe, R.N. "There you are!" Lilah said the second she spied Wade. "I don't care how many times you duck my calls, you are not getting out of our talk, Wade McCabe." Saved by the Mom, Josie thought.

Wade sighed loudly and regarded Lilah with a mixture of chagrin and affection. Josie thought, amused, Wade had seen this coming a mile away.

"No, Mom, I don't expect that I will," Wade drawled affectionately. He winked at his mother, patted her on the shoulder and bent to kiss her cheek. "But I can sure as heck put it off a bit…say till the next time I'm out at the ranch with you and Dad. Meanwhile, I'm heading back to my ranch to go over the latest geology reports and core samples with Josie here." Wade curved a surprisingly proprietary hand over her shoulder.

"Josie, say hi to my mom," he quipped.

Before the two women could even finish exchanging hellos and nods, Wade hustled Josie out the door.

"No son of mine has turned into a heartbreaker yet, and if I have my way, none of you ever will!" Lilah called after Wade.

Wade chuckled and gave his mother a deferential nod but did not slow his steps, nor did he allow Josie to slow hers as they turned the corner and headed toward the door to the parking lot behind the hospital.

"What did your mother mean by that?" Josie asked in a low, humor-filled tone. She paused, manila contract file pressed to her chest, then continued wryly, "Or shouldn't I ask?"

Many men wouldn't have answered such an intimate question. Not Wade.

He released an exasperated sigh. "She thinks I don't give women a chance."

Alarm bells went off in Josie's head. "Let me guess," she said dryly, casting him a probing sidelong glance. "And you think you do."

"Let me put it this way." Wade held the door for her, then followed her out into the bright sunshine. "I know a sure thing when I see it." He reached for his sunglasses the same time Josie reached for hers. "And by the same token," he said as he walked her toward her Wyatt Drilling Company pickup truck, "I know a bad match, too. When it becomes obvious something isn't right, I don't waste my time or hers."

Josie swallowed as they skirted their way between the rows of parked cars and trucks. "Meaning, you dump them."

Her tone was contentious, but he refused to take the bait. "I prefer to think of it as being honest," Wade said calmly.

"How do they see it?" Shifting the folder to her other arm, Josie reached into her pocket for her keys.

Wade shrugged his broad shoulders laconically. "I'm sure they're grateful to me in the long run, when they've had a chance to think it over."

Josie inserted her key in the lock. "In other words, they're mad as hell."

"They don't have any right to be." Wade watched her swing the driver side door open and roll down that window as a wave of heat rushed out, engulfing them both. "Especially since I usually take the time and trouble to point out the reason or reasons why we're all wrong for each other."

Deciding the interior of the truck was much too hot to get in, Josie tossed her folder on the bench seat, then moved around the back of the truck to the passenger side. She opened the door and rolled that window down, too. "I'm sure that goes over like a lead balloon," Josie muttered, recalling when that very indignity had happened to her, not so long ago. Finished, she turned to face Wade and propped her hands on her hips. "Just out of curiosity, who is usually at fault in this situation?" And was his mother right to worry he was becoming a heartbreaker?

Wade regarded Josie with barely veiled amusement. "I don't like to assign blame."

"Of course not," Josie countered sweetly, rolling her eyes. Was this shifting into a flirtation?

He lifted an indolent hand. "It's more like a Cinderella thing," he explained with comically exaggerated seriousness. "You know, when the glass slipper doesn't fit, it just doesn't."

In no hurry to be on her way, now that the conversation had gotten really interesting, Josie lifted her face to his. "Give me an example, anyway."

Wade took her hand and led her toward one of the trees shading the perimeter of the parking lot. He stepped into the shade, taking her right along with him, before finally dropping her hand from his. "Suppose you and I were dating and you never wore anything but jeans and T-shirts, no matter where we went or what we did."

Glad she had her sunglasses on to shade the fiery temper in her eyes, Josie flattened her palms behind her and leaned back against the trunk. "As it happens," Josie interrupted dryly, looking up at Wade McCabe, "these days, I usually don't."

Wade shrugged and kept his gaze trained on hers. "I'd probably drop a few hints—"

"Which," Josie said just as decisively, "I'd ignore."

The corners of Wade's sensually chiseled lips inched upward. "And then, that being the case, I'd probably tell you that you're taking the Texas tomboy thing a little too far."

There was nothing Josie hated more than unsolicited advice.

Especially since her relationship with Ben had ended because he had—in the end—disapproved of her, too.

"Then I'd probably remind you that, as a general rule, you'll never get the guys by being one of them 100 percent of the time."

"Has it occurred to you I might not want to get the guys, as you so tactfully put it?" Josie said hotly. In fact, right now she had no interest in having a boyfriend, period! Which made it stranger still to feel the tingles of awareness starting up inside her, whenever Wade was near.

"Yes. In fact, I sensed that about you right away." Wade took off his sunglasses and looked her up and down, giving her an up-close view of his beautiful dark brown eyes. "I just can't figure out why."

"Fortunately for both of us," Josie returned haughtily, trying not to notice the way his hot glance was skimming her from head to toe, "you have no need to know."

Silence fell between them, and a warm breeze wafted over them, as Wade continued to study her beneath the deep blue Texas sky. "What does your family think about this job of yours, anyway?" he asked finally in a soft, seductive tone.

Suffused with heat everywhere his eyes had touched, Josie swallowed and turned her glance away. How was it this man, whom she had just met, instinctively knew so much about her? She wasn't used to anyone being that clued in!

She looked into his eyes with all the directness she could muster. "My parents would rather I have nothing to do with roughnecks and drilling for oil, and instead wish I would marry some nice man and settle down and have a family, pronto," she replied, ending with a soft, beleaguered sigh. In fact, both had been incessantly urging her to do just that for six months now.

"So," Wade said slyly, "why don't you?"

Chapter 3

Josie hesitated. She didn't want to talk about Ben and the heartbreak he had caused her. Never mind how devastating it had been to once again know she hadn't quite measured up in the eyes of someone she loved. And worse, probably never could. Not in Ben's eyes and not in her parents'.

Aware Wade was waiting for an answer, Josie lifted her gaze to his. "It's not like I don't want to get married someday," she said eventually, as the warm June breeze stirred the air around her. "I do."

"But...?" Wade rested a palm on the tree trunk beside her.

Josie tried not to think how much his nearness disturbed her. He was close enough she could feel his body heat and breathe in the sandalwood and leather scent of soap and cologne, close enough to feel the undeniable sizzle of sexual attraction between them. Aware that her heart was racing and her knees were trembling slightly at the way he was towering over her, she shrugged and let her eyes rove over his tall, solidly built frame and broad, powerful shoulders.

"First I have a lot to prove," she said matter-of-factly, her cheeks warming slightly as she held his steady, probing gaze.

"Such as…?" he murmured casually, moving closer yet.

Sensing that this Texas playboy could—and would—be dangerous to her heart if given half a chance, Josie unlocked their gazes. She was not going to permit another man to break her heart and make her question everything, she reminded herself firmly as she fortified herself against his tantalizing grin.

"That I can lead an independent life of my own choosing. That I can be who I'm meant to be without any interference from anyone else. And speaking of that independent life—" Josie glanced at her watch—she had dawdled far too long as it was "—I'd better get on back to the rig before Gus and the guys begin to wonder what's happened to me."

"I'll be right behind you," Wade promised lazily. Josie shot him a curious glance as he stepped back, allowing her to move away from the trees shading the perimeter of the parking lot. "Now that we're going to continue drilling," he said easily, falling into step beside her as she approached her now-somewhat-cooled-off pickup truck, "I want to have a look at the latest core samples and the logs."

"No problem," Josie replied. Hopefully he'd be as

enthusiastic as she was, once he had the chance to study them.

Wade hopped in his black Ford Expedition and she could see him in her rearview as he followed her through town, staying with her the entire twenty miles to the property he'd purchased just a few months ago.

Had he tried, Josie thought as they turned into the narrow gravel lane, he couldn't have picked a more incongruous piece of property. Topographically, of course, the Golden Slipper Ranch was much the same as other ranches in the area. The ten-thousand-acre property was comprised of gently rolling hills, vast flat meadows and several meandering creeks. But there all resemblance stopped. Instead of the usual rustic ranch house and barns, and numerous horse or cattle pastures, was a small, hopelessly feminine country cottage with all sorts of gingerbread trim. Josie had never been inside it, as the Wyatt Drilling Company trailers, the derrick and discovery well were located on the opposite end of the property. But as they zoomed past it, Josie wondered if the ranch house was as frou-frou inside as it looked to be on the outside. And if so, would Wade McCabe want that changed, if he ever decided to live out there? Or had the purchase been just another business transaction to the millionaire investor and Laramie, Texas, native? Josie knew—from their business records—that Wade McCabe already maintained both a home and an office in Houston and had for some time, as well as numerous other "investment properties" around the state.

Unfortunately, no sooner had they pulled up next to the old derrick, than the huge rotary drill began to make a hideous grinding sound, sort of like tires that were stuck and spinning in the sand. Simultaneously the alarm on the derrick began to sound. To Josie's chagrin, Ernie and Dieter were already running in their direction, but Gus—her father's highly valued old hand and resident tool and drilling expert—was nowhere in sight.

Wade vaulted from his truck, knowing as did she that the alarm meant trouble with a capital *T*. "This is exactly what I was afraid of, now that Big Jim is not around!"

"Not to worry, cowboy," Josie shouted, jumping down from the cab of her battered blue Wyatt Drilling pickup truck. Aware she was closer than anyone else, she raced up the metal steps leading to the drilling platform. "I know exactly what to do!"

With Wade hard on her heels, Josie raced across the metal floor and yanked the lever that shut down the drill. An ear-splitting whine pierced the air as the heavy machinery ground to a halt, then all fell silent once again.

Josie caught her breath as Dieter and Ernie joined her on the high metal platform.

"Damn drill keeps getting hung up," Dieter complained to Josie.

His expression concerned, Ernie added, "We hit another pocket of sand and gravel. It keeps caving in on the drill and clogging things up, which in turn stops the drilling."

"The cuttings are probably slipping past your desander and staying in suspension in your drilling mud,"

Josie said "If Big Jim were here he'd tell you to clean your pits and mix new mud."

"It'll cost time," Dieter argued.

"In the short run, but not the long run," Josie advised calmly.

Gus, who'd been off on an errand, arrived in time to hear the tail end of the discussion. "Josie's right," he said as he joined the group assembled around the drill. "So let's get started."

Leaving Gus to supervise, Josie and Wade headed back over to the trailer, which had been set up as an on-site office.

"Where'd you learn all that?" Wade asked, amazed.

Josie shrugged, belatedly aware she might have looked a little too competent just now, as she got out the logs detailing rates of penetration, shut-down time, weight on bit, trip time and how much torque was being used to turn the bit. She laid them out for Wade to peruse.

"I picked it up, I guess."

He thumbed through a couple of pages, his attention more on her than the meticulously detailed drilling records in front of him. "In Dallas-Fort Worth?"

Josie could see, like it or not, she was going to have to tell him a little more about herself. "My parents divorced when I was just a baby," she admitted uncomfortably, going to the cabinet to get out the samples of the rock they'd been drilling through, as well. "My dad was a roughneck, and whenever I spent time with him, I also spent time at the drilling sites." She added the latest geological surveys to the stack, then edged around behind the desk to check for messages that had come in while she was out.

"How did your mom feel about that?" Wade asked, watching as Josie picked up a stack of pink papers imprinted with the header While You Were Out.

Josie scanned the messages quickly. Noting three of the five calls were from her mother, she made a face. She really did not want to speak to Bitsy at this moment.

Aware Wade was still waiting for her to answer, Josie replied, "She didn't like it but there was nothing she could do about it. The court ordered I spend summers and most vacations with my father, and that's always where he was. And speaking of mothers, shouldn't you be running off to talk with yours just about now?"

"Don't remind me." Wade grinned at her unrepentantly. "The lecture on why I should ease up on women and just pick a bride is one I can do without. But you're right," he said dryly, consulting his watch, "I should go see them. Just not for the reason you think."

Lilah and John McCabe were already in the hospital conference room with one of Houston's most sought-after photographers when Wade arrived to watch the portrait taking. "I still don't think this is really necessary," Lilah said to Wade, as she straightened her white nurse's uniform and the pink cardigan she habitually wore with it.

"Same here," John, who was wearing a shirt and tie and lab coat, grumbled.

Wade dropped into a contoured chair. He smiled as his parents allowed the photographer to seat them in front of the blue screen. "The portrait of the two of you will be a nice addition to the lobby," he said.

"Oh, please," John and Lilah rolled their eyes in unison. "No one is going to want our portrait in the lobby."

Wade lifted a dissenting brow as he steepled his fingers together in front of him. "You're wrong about that. Everyone in Laramie knows you two are the reason this hospital even exists," Wade said. John and Lilah had fought hard to make their dream a reality. As a result, everyone in Laramie and the surrounding rural community had benefited.

John winked at Lilah mischievously. "I suppose we could hang it in the staff lounge and let the staff throw darts at it."

Lilah tossed back her head and laughed as the photographer snapped their photos in quick successions. It wasn't the dignified photo session—or portrait of his parents—he'd envisioned, but maybe it was better his folks be remembered this way, Wade thought. As the fun-loving, hard-working, giving and affectionate people they were.

"So how are the plans for the bridal shower coming, Mom?" Wade asked casually as the photographer guided his parents into another pose.

"It's going to be held at Remington's Bar & Grill on Saturday evening," Lilah reported happily as she slipped her hands around John's waist. She leaned her cheek against her husband's shoulder. "We've rented out the whole place!"

John wrapped one hand around Lilah's waist, and tucked his other beneath her chin, lifting her face to his. "From what I hear it's going to be a little wild," he teased.

Lilah blushed as she gazed up at him adoringly. "I'm sure those are just rumors, John."

"Mmm-hmm." John grinned at his wife disbelievingly then mugged for the photographer. While Wade watched, the photographer snapped several more photos before turning Lilah away from John, her back to John's chest, her head resting against his shoulder. "That'll be the day! Especially when the Lockhart girls are all expected back for it!"

Lilah nestled contentedly against her husband. "It'll be nice to have them all in town again," she murmured as more photos were snapped.

"Speaking of which, Wade," Lilah continued slyly, "none of the Lockhart girls are married now, either."

"I know what you're thinking, and you can doggone well forget it, both of you!" Wade said sternly, as he thought of the four feisty, spirited, beautiful, wonderful women he'd grown up with. Unfortunately it didn't make a difference how attractive the Lockhart women were. They'd played together from the time they were toddlers on. "The Lockhart girls were like sisters to all of us," Wade reminded his parents. Even if they had lately—because of the various directions their lives had all taken—begun to lose touch with each other.

"One of them may have a friend who is just right for you," Lilah persisted.

Wade paused, his curiosity getting the better of him. "I know Meg's a nurse and just got back to town, and Jenna's designing dresses. What are Kelsey and Dani up to these days?"

"Dani is a theater and movie critic for the San Antonio newspaper. She's supposedly quite good, although she is roundly criticized for her reviews of romance. Apparently, she's never seen even one—drama or comedy!—that she's liked yet," Lilah supplied with a sigh. "And according to her sisters she's equally cynical and hypercritical when it comes to men."

Wade ran a hand across his jaw. "I don't remember her being that way in high school. In fact, she was almost boy crazy, wasn't she?"

Lilah and John nodded in unison.

"So something must have happened to turn her against romance," Wade theorized bluntly.

"Unfortunately, no one knows what it is," Lilah said.

Wade figured whatever had happened must have been significant: the Dani he recalled had never been one to hold a grudge against anyone, never mind the whole male gender.

"What about Kelsey?" Wade asked, as the photographer posed Lilah and John yet again.

Lilah sighed as she exchanged concerned looks with her husband.

"Kelsey is still something of a ne'er-do-well, I'm afraid."

Wade remembered Kelsey as the pampered baby of the family and the life of every party.

John nodded, adding, "Despite the fact her sisters have been very supportive of her every venture, Kelsey's never yet stuck with anything for more than a few months at a time. Her latest plan is to somehow get back the ranch their parents owned when they were alive."

Wade watched as the photographer stepped back to his camera and focused the lens on his camera. "Does Kelsey know anything about ranching?" Wade asked curiously as the flash went off and another picture was snapped.

"Not a lick. But you know Kelsey," Lilah said dryly as she smiled and looked directly into the camera's lens. "That won't keep her from trying."

Wade knew that was true. Kelsey Lockhart was as mule-headed and impulsive as could be.

The photographer grinned. "I think I've got it, folks."

"Great!" Lilah and John said in unison. As the photographer began to dismantle his equipment, Lilah headed straight for Wade. "As long as you're in town, honey, I want you to join your father and me for dinner tonight. And I'd like you to bring a date. So—"

"No problem." Wade interrupted his mother smoothly, knowing a potential fix-up when he saw one. "I already had plans to ask someone to dinner, anyway."

Lilah lifted a skeptical brow. "Not your usual ditzy society belle, I hope?" John remarked.

Lilah elbowed John in the ribs, giving the signal to use more tact, even as she tried again. "What your father means, dear, is we're not sure your kind of glitzy woman would be comfortable with the kind of down-home supper at the ranch your father and I have planned for this evening. So maybe you should let us arrange a partner for you…."

Not while he still had a breath left in him! Wade thought. "The lady I have in mind will be happy with any kind of home-cooked meal," he said.

* * *

Later, at the trailer, Wade waited for Josie to answer him. Glossy dark brown tendrils were escaping from her ponytail to frame her delicate oval face. She had a big smudge of grease across her cheek and red ink—from the pen she had been using—slashed across her temple. Dirt from the drilling rig's mud pit stained her jeans and splattered her red western boots. Perspiration dampened her T-shirt in the middle of her back, between her breasts and across her taut sexy midriff. If you discarded her pink hard hat covered with stenciled-on daisies, she looked like a kid who'd gotten hot and dirty making mud pies.

"You did hear me, didn't you?" Wade asked, when another minute passed and she still didn't speak.

Josie blinked. She swept off her hat, lifted her arm and wiped the sweat from her brow with the inside of her wrist. "You want to take me to dinner at your parents' ranch?" she repeated in a low, deadpan voice. "Tonight...?"

Wade shrugged. "That's what I said."

Josie propped both hands on her hips and shot him a mildly rebuking look. "Why?" she asked, as if she were still waiting for the punch line.

Wade let his glance rove the flushed, golden skin of her face. He didn't know why he felt the one-two jab of physical attraction—she wasn't at all his type—but he did. "Why not?" he shot back.

Josie scowled as if she found it an insult just to receive the invitation. "I don't have anything to wear."

"Believe me, what you're wearing is just fine." In fact, he'd like nothing better than to show up with her,

as is, to get his matchmaking mother off his back once
and for all.

Josie tossed her hard hat onto the desk with a clatter.
With a few choice words Wade was pretty sure he was
meant not just to hear but to take to heart, she ripped
the bandana from around her neck and used it to mop
her face. A muscle ticking in her elegantly boned cheek,
she regarded him suspiciously. "You—Mr. Discrimi-
nating about His Women to the Nth Degree—want me
to look like this when you take me home to dinner?"

Wade nodded, aware he liked the tartness in her
voice almost as much as the fiery indignation in her
blue eyes. "Right."

Her lips forming a soft, delectable pout, Josie
stepped forward contentiously, until the two of them
were standing toe-to-toe. She angled her chin up, the
better to look into his face. "What's really going on
here?" she demanded in a low, furious tone.

Wade rubbed his jaw laconically. Then, aware she
was still watching him carefully, he shrugged as if to
say why should anything have to be going on? Holding her steady gaze with ever-escalating pleasure,
he drawled, "Given how hard y'all have been working around here, I figured maybe you could do with a
home-cooked meal."

He hadn't figured she'd react this way to a simple
request for her company. Women usually climbed all
over each other and stood in line to get a date with him.
He didn't kid himself—he knew it was as much for the
money in his bank accounts as anything else—but even
without that he wouldn't have had any trouble getting a

date. Until now, anyway. With this one very sexy, very feisty, Texas tomboy.

"And maybe that would be true if I didn't think you had an ulterior motive that doesn't have a damn thing to do with helping me," Josie shot back, even more sweetly.

"Outspoken little thing, aren't you?"

Josie blushed fiercely. "I'm not little—except compared to Texas-size men like you." She studied the length of his six-foot-five, two-hundred-twenty-pound frame. "And this has something to do with that talk your mother wanted to have with you, doesn't it?"

Abruptly, Wade figured he might as well level with her. It was the only way he'd get her to go out with him. And suddenly he very much wanted her to go out with him. "My folks both want me to date less glitzy women." And go for women of substance. Women he could possibly fall in love with, instead of women who wouldn't hold his interest for more than a few days— or nights—at the very most. "Tonight, I'm giving them their wish."

"What a thoughtful person you are," Josie retorted in a low, deadpan voice.

"I like to think so," Wade agreed sagely. He'd found out the hard way that he wasn't cut out for the kind of emotional intimacy needed to sustain a relationship. It had been a painful revelation. He wasn't going through that again. Nor would he put anyone else through the same. Luckily for him, Josie appeared every bit as interested in business and uninterested in romance as he was.

"And the answer is…"

Wade was sure Josie was about to say no when Gus came striding in.

Josie looked at Gus, colored slightly, then turned to Wade. "Yes," she said swiftly. "I'd be happy to go to dinner with you."

Wade stared at Josie with only slightly less astonishment than Gus. Clearly, both had expected her to refuse the invitation to date a client. And under normal circumstances, Josie thought, she wouldn't be. But like it or not these weren't normal circumstances. She'd only had to look at Gus's face as he'd entered the trailer to know that Gus'd heard all about the latest in a series of problems with the drilling and that Gus had had an attack of conscience and would spill all to Wade—promptly!—unless she did something lightning quick. "Just give me a second to talk to Gus in private and let me get cleaned up and then I'll be right with you."

"I'll wait here, if it's okay with you," Wade said.

Josie nodded. She went to a shelf and brought back copies of the latest seismic survey of the ranch for him to peruse. "I'll make it as fast as I can," she promised. Gus on her heels, she headed out the door and down the steps.

Together they crossed the dusty ground to the trailer where Josie was bunking for the duration.

"Just what do you think you're doing?" Gus demanded with the familiarity of an old family friend.

"Keeping the door open for success is what it looks like," Josie said. Darn it all, she'd come too far and done too much to quit now. She couldn't pull something like this and fail and then face her phenomenally successful father—it would just be too much!

"It isn't just our hides at stake here, Josie." Gus followed Josie into her air-conditioned living trailer. "Big Jim's reputation is on the line, too."

"Don't you think I know that?" Josie shot right back emotionally. "Don't you think I want my father to be proud of me?" It seemed she had waited her whole life for that to happen! And the same went for her mother, too.

She knew she had crossed the line in even accepting this job in her father's absence. He'd left her in charge in name only, not in any real fashion. Yet she also knew if she were successful she would receive kudos for her actions. She looked at Gus imploringly, more determined than ever to succeed. "Look, just don't do or say anything to blow this," she pleaded softly as she kicked off her mud-caked boots and—for lack of a better place—washed them off in the kitchen sink. "Not now. Not when we've come so far. I meant what I told him earlier." Finished, Josie vigorously toweled off her boots with a paper towel and said passionately, "We're close to striking oil here, Gus. I can feel it in my bones."

"That's exactly what your father always says," Gus murmured, shaking his head. "He gets that very same look in his eyes."

Josie pleaded, "Just hold out a little while longer."

Gus glanced out the window at the drilling rig. "We've just had so many problems on this one, Josie—"

"Wade McCabe is totally cool with all that," Josie replied mulishly, as she rushed around, trying to find her last clean pair of jeans and a shirt. "If he wasn't, would he have agreed to let us continue drilling or be taking me to dinner at his family ranch?"

Gus scowled suspiciously and rubbed at the back of his leathery neck. "I don't know."

"Well, I do!" Josie threw her arms around him and kissed Gus's cheek. "This is all going to be fine in the end," she told him enthusiastically. "Better than fine! You'll see!"

Giving him no chance to argue with her further, she shooed him out, then headed for the shower. Ten minutes later she was dressed again and heading out to meet Wade. His glance slid over her old, faded jeans and equally faded—but clean—red denim work shirt.

"Get whatever you needed to, settled with Gus?" he asked, almost too casually.

Josie looked up at Gus, who was standing on the drilling rig platform and talking to Ernie and Dieter and still regarding Josie and Wade as if he was worried.

"Gus just wanted to make sure I knew what I was doing when it came to you and me." Josie paused. "I told him I did."

Wade looked at her steadily.

"And that was all?"

Josie struggled against the sudden wish to tell him everything. She gave Wade her most innocent look. "What else could it be?"

Although visibly surprised to see the denim-clad Josie arrive with Wade, instead of some dolled-up society lady, John and Lilah welcomed Josie into their home with the warm hospitality that had become their trademark in the community.

Then John winked at Josie—who was still none too sure she'd done the right thing in accompanying Wade here, even if it had gotten her away from Gus and his second thoughts!—and turned back to Wade. "Your mother and I know there isn't a situation in the world you think you can't handle," he drawled, prodding his son deliberately, "but this may be it."

"Underestimating me a tad, aren't you?" Wade returned.

Lilah sized up the situation with equal aplomb. A knowing smile on her face, Lilah wiped her hands on the apron around her middle, then linked her arm through Josie's. "Come with me, honey. You can help with dinner."

"I'd love to help however I can," Josie said as she walked with Lilah through the wide, wooden-floored hallway. She felt immediately at home in the McCabe's sprawling, rustically decorated ranch house. "The only problem is—I can't cook." Her repertoire to date included iced tea with sliced lemon—a southern staple—and not much else. Unless you counted cold cereal with milk and peanut butter or lunch meat sandwiches.

Lilah handed Josie a denim apron from a hook behind the door. "All you have to do is stir the gravy. Nothing to it," Lilah soothed, unperturbed, as she began removing pieces of crusty golden chicken-fried steak from the big cast-iron skillet on the stove and laid them on a platter. "I'll talk you through it," she promised, as she slid the steak into the oven to stay warm.

Lilah sprinkled several tablespoons of flour into the drippings in the pan. Handing Josie a wooden spoon, she pointed her toward the cast-iron skillet and motioned for her to begin stirring.

"So, how did that son of mine talk you into this?" Lilah asked, going to the refrigerator for milk and butter. "What exactly did he offer you to entice you to let yourself be used this way?"

A reprieve from Gus's censuring gaze, Josie thought, as she stirred the flour into the drippings and watched as the mixture turned a smooth, bubbling brown. "What makes you think Wade offered me anything except the pleasure of his company and a chance at a home-cooked meal?" Josie asked Lilah.

Lilah tested the potatoes with a fork. She smiled with satisfaction as the potatoes fell apart. "Because I know my son, and he thinks the world revolves around money and business success for him and everyone else. Bottom line, he has to come out ahead financially and otherwise in literally every situation or he is unhappy."

Josie could see that was true.

"Worse, he is convinced he has a Midas touch," Lilah continued as she lifted the pan off the stove and poured the steaming potatoes into a colander to drain.

"Does he?" Josie kept stirring as the mixture in the skillet got thicker and thicker.

"Up till now—without peril. At least in his business life. His personal life is another matter." Lilah grabbed the milk and poured some in Josie's skillet. The thick smooth roux immediately became lumpy again, prompting Josie to stir even harder. "Which is why I think you should stay clear of my son, Josie, at least for the moment."

Wade strolled in. "You told her not to date me?"

Lilah turned on the hand mixer and began to mash the potatoes. "In a nutshell, yes. Though it pains me to admit this—" she paused to add milk and butter to the potatoes, "—I don't think you've yet learned to treat women with the gentility and deference they deserve."

John joined them, too. He lifted a lid on the stove and gave the simmering green beans a stir. "Although, in our son's defense, it's not as if he never knew how to treat a woman. Wade was a fine gentleman till he met Sandra."

Wade's mouth tightened instantly. He glared at his dad. "I thought we agreed never to talk about that again!"

Josie wouldn't have minded. She wanted to know more about the woman who'd had a lasting impact on Wade McCabe.

Lilah finished whipping the potatoes and turned off her mixer with a resounding click. "If it weren't still hurting you, I wouldn't," she said stubbornly.

Wade filled glasses with iced water and carried them to the kitchen table, which had been draped with a pretty blue-and-white-checkered tablecloth. A bouquet of flowers sat in a stoneware crock on the center of the table.

"It isn't hurting me," Wade pushed the words through a row of white, even teeth.

"Oh, really." Lilah brought out the tossed salad and began to dress it with balsamic vinegar and oil. "Then why is every female you've brought home in the last five years a shallow debutante or heiress?"

At the mention of debutantes and heiresses, Josie went very still. Guilt flooded her, making her cheeks turn alternately red and white. "You've got something against debutantes and heiresses?" Josie asked Lilah casually, remembering finally to give the cream gravy bubbling in the skillet another desultory stir.

Lilah smiled at Josie gently as she began to transfer the steaming food to serving dishes. "Not per se," she replied gently, "just the ones who haven't an earnest thought in their heads. And those are the only kind he's brought home! I might as well say it, Wade McCabe. I want to see you and the rest of your brothers married."

"So work on them," Wade said, making no effort to mask his exasperation.

"I am," Lilah replied.

Wade wrinkled his nose as something noxious began to compete with the delicious aroma of steak and potatoes. "What is that awful smell?" he demanded.

"Oh, my heavens!" Lilah looked down at the smoking skillet.

Josie followed Lilah's gaze and groaned. She'd done it again.

"I'm sorry about the gravy," Josie told Wade as he parked his truck in front of her trailer.

Wade vaulted out and came around to help her with her door. "Stop apologizing." He grasped her hand and helped her down from the truck. "We didn't need it, anyway."

Josie tossed her head and sent him a rueful look.

"That's kind of you to say, but you know as well as I do that chicken-fried steak without cream gravy is like an ice-cream cone without the ice cream."

Wade shrugged his broad shoulders. He looked handsome and imposing in the early-evening light. And in absolutely no hurry to go home. "So we saved ourselves a few calories," he drawled in a husky baritone that sent shudders of acute awareness racing up and down Josie's spine.

Josie slowed her stride as they approached the concrete steps leading up to her front door. For reasons she couldn't begin to fathom, she was reluctant to go in. Reluctant for the unexpectedly delightful evening to end. She bit into her lower lip. "I suppose."

As they paused in front of the steps, Wade reached up and smoothed a tendril of hair from her cheek. "My parents really liked you," he said gently.

Josie nodded. She cast a look at the crescent moon, already visible in the dusky sky above, before returning her gaze to Wade's face. "I like them. They're very nice people."

He turned to her, his shoulder nudging hers as he moved. "You going to take them up on their offer and have dinner out at the ranch without me?" he asked in the same soft, self-confident voice.

She met his eyes and with effort overcame the quivers of desire starting deep inside her. Wondering if he was going to try and kiss her good-night before she slipped inside, as well as what she'd do if he did, she asked, "Would it bother you if I did?"

The corners of Wade's lips turned up in a slow, sensual smile. "In a way, yeah—maybe because it's the first time they've ever liked my date more than they liked me."

Josie flushed self-consciously as her heart took on a slow, thudding beat. "I'm sure that's not true."

A glimmer of humor sparkled in Wade's eyes before he turned his attention to the UPS box wedged just inside the screen door. "Looks like you've got a package."

Glad for the diversion—maybe it would make her stop secretly wishing he'd haul her in his arms and kiss her!—Josie leaned forward and retrieved the package. "It's a care package from my mother," Josie murmured, covering up the return name and address with her hand. Worse, she had an idea exactly what was inside. And knew with a certainty as solid as gold that the contents were nothing Wade should see. "Maybe it'll have some clean clothes in it," she joked, holding the thick rectangular mailing box to her chest. "And speaking of laundry, I better get a move on if I'm going to get any done tonight."

Wade grinned and regarded her mischievously, his lively dark brown eyes alight with interest. "Not inviting me in, hmm?"

Josie shook her head. "Thanks for dinner." Giving him no chance to protest, she slipped inside. She waited till he headed back toward his Expedition, then opened the box. Inside was just what she'd thought—a beautiful evening gown, exactly her style, and just right for the summer social season.

It had been so long since she'd worn anything so ridiculously frou-frou and feminine. Her mother was right, Josie thought wistfully as she ran her fingers across the sheer, pale mauve silk. She didn't miss the endless whirl of glittering social events and the pressure to look incredibly beautiful at each and every event, but she did miss feeling like a woman, dressing up. Since she'd started working for Wyatt Drilling she'd hardly worn anything but jeans.

Josie wondered with amusement what Wade McCabe would think if he saw her in this. Laughing softly, she shook her head and held the dress up to herself wistfully, peered into the mirror on the back of the open bathroom door. And that was when she saw Wade McCabe, standing just on the other side of the screen door, watching her.

Chapter 4

Figuring she had no recourse but to brazen her way through this sticky situation, Josie held the enormously expensive evening gown up to herself in the mirror, then turned ever so slowly and looked at Wade.

"No doubt about it," she quipped, tongue in cheek. "Mother has outdone herself this time." She sighed, secretly regretting the fact she'd never have any place to wear the incredibly gorgeous gown, at least not in the near future. And carefully put the elegant dress, embroidered with finely beaded garlands of tiny pink petals and long flowing vines, back down in the folds of tissue.

Wade stepped inside, file folder in hand, the reason for his unexpected return evident. Wordlessly he handed her the legal papers she'd accidentally left in his truck, then swept off his hat and held it to his chest.

His glance dipped briefly to the dress before returning to her. "You don't like it?"

Josie's breath hitched in her chest as she tilted her face up to his. Just being near him again made her heart skip a beat. "It's obviously not for me."

He dropped his hat on the sofa and swaggered closer, his steps long and lazy. "How do you know unless you try it on?" he asked huskily.

Josie's eyes focused on the wispy ash-brown curls springing from the open collar of his shirt. "Don't be ridiculous." She couldn't wear a dress like that around the drilling site! And she'd look equally ridiculous wearing it around her utilitarian Wyatt Drilling Company trailer.

Wade leaned closer. His warm breath whispered across her ear. "Afraid you'll like it, huh?" His voice was sexy, self-assured and faintly baiting.

Josie swallowed and stepped back. "Of course not."

A slow, sexy smile spread across the ruggedly handsome contours of his face. "Then try it on," Wade dared.

Josie looked into his eyes. She knew he thought she wouldn't dare. And it was the challenge in his brown eyes that prodded her to behave just as foolishly and impetuously as he was.

"Fine, but when I do you'll see what I've already told you—this dress is just not for me, not by a long shot." She picked up the box, cradled it to her chest and swept toward the bedroom.

"I don't know about that," Wade called after her, his gaze moving up and down the length of her. "I think it could be. Given the right circumstances."

Josie rolled her eyes. "Well, the right circumstances aren't likely to come along out here," she said stubbornly.

"You never know." Wade sauntered closer and stood, arms folded in front of him, leaning against the door frame. "Besides, it never hurts to be prepared," he said as he watched Josie perch on the end of her bed and kick off her boots. His brown eyes lit up merrily. "Say, for instance, if we were to strike oil by week's end. I might just fly you and the rest of the guys to Houston in my Lear jet to celebrate in style." He smiled as if he'd like nothing better, then wagged a finger her way. "If that's the case, then you will be needing the dress."

With effort Josie shelved the mental image of the two of them painting the town red. Although she enjoyed the finer things in life as much as the next person, she didn't need them in order to be happy, never had. "When we strike oil, a dinner at the local diner would be fine."

"I doubt Gus, Ernie and Dieter would be so quick to dismiss my offer, even if it required they wear a dinner jacket."

Probably not, Josie thought, struggling not to notice how good Wade looked in his tight-fitting jeans, boots, light blue shirt and stone-colored sport coat, or how ruggedly at ease.

Deciding he'd seen quite enough of her bedroom— with its mussed bed and heaps of dirty clothes fighting for space among the stacks of country and western compact discs and geology and drilling handbooks— Josie vaulted to her feet and hop-skipped her way to the door. Hand to his chest, she pushed him back, knowing if a point was to be made this was indeed the very best way to make it. "Have a seat on the sofa out there, cowboy. I'll be out directly."

Deliberately leaving her hair in the mussy ponytail on the back of her head, Josie quickly divested herself of her jeans and faded red denim shirt. She had only to look at the low, scooped front and back of the sleeveless gown to know it would not work with any bra she had with her. So, reluctantly she dropped that, too. Then, clad in socks and panties, she slipped into the sexy gown and zipped it to mid-spine.

The glittering gown swirling around her, she moved toward the full-length mirror nailed to the back of the closet door. As suspected, the gown was a perfect fit. As for the rest—Josie sighed and shook her head as she looked at her sunburned face in the mirror.

As much as Josie hated to admit it, her mother was also right about this: the weeks spent working out in the Texas sun had wreaked havoc with her hair, nails and skin. Her long brown hair was no longer in perfect condition. Her cheeks and nose were sunburned, her lips chapped and dry. And darn it all, there was a part of her, a small part, that did regret looking like this.

She'd been cultivating an image of a Texas tomboy to add to her own credibility as an up-and-coming, independent oil woman and wildcatter in her own right, and to a point she had enjoyed keeping the grooming routine ultrasimple, and not having to worry about anything except showering and putting on a set of fresh clothes every day. But there was another part of her—a deeper, womanly part—that missed wearing makeup and pretty clothes, a part of her that missed the long, fragrant bubble baths she used to take, and the time to do something with her hair.

There was a part of her that missed the occasional night on the town, the chance to feel beautiful and eat a good meal, have a glass of wine and dance in a man's arms.

But Wade McCabe could not know any of that, Josie warned herself. What he had to see was a woman who would *never* be the perfect lady of his dreams.

So Josie left her thick white socks on and kept her hair in the unkempt ponytail. Forgoing even the tiniest hint of makeup or lip gloss, she squared her slender shoulders, pivoted and made her way around her cluttered bedroom to the door. She yanked it open and then walked as ungracefully as possible out into the room.

Knowing she looked ridiculously dowdy in the glittering dress, Josie expected Wade McCabe to take one look at her and burst out into uncontrollable laughter. Instead, his eyes darkened and his powerful chest rose and lowered as he took a long, deep breath. His brown eyes still locked with hers, looking like he'd just found the most beautiful girl in the world—or at the very least a gem in the rough—he stood and came slowly toward her.

Wade had expected Josie to look good in the glitzy gown, but not this good, he thought as she stomped toward him cantankerously, her thick white socks making soft, thudding noises across the scuffed-up tile floor. The neckline of her dress was lower in front and in back than he had imagined, scooping down to reveal a good three inches of shadowy décolletage and creamy white breasts. A garland of pale pink petals draped the entire neckline of Josie's gown, drawing attention to her slender shoulders and sexy arms, her equally feminine and impressive bare back. The sheer, clinging silk caressed her taut midriff like a lover's caress, before sliding down across her hips and swirling sexily past her knees to the floor. Wade had only to see her move and zero in on the soft, jiggling motions of her breasts beneath the thin silk and the raised imprint of her nipples to know she had dispensed with her bra, right along with her shirt and jeans. In fact, just looking at her made his heart pound and his mouth water.

Not that she had done anything specific to entice him, he thought, as she marched toward him in a drift of her everyday orange blossom perfume. She hadn't combed her hair. She didn't have on a lick of makeup. She wasn't wearing the sexy shoes or the glittering jewels the dress demanded. And yet she was, without a doubt, the most beautiful woman he had ever seen.

So beautiful he found himself wondering what she would look like if she had taken the time and energy to seduce him. And that being the case, he thought, as she ground stubbornly to a halt just in front of him and he lifted a hand to her face, he might as well indulge his curiosity just a bit.

"What are you doing?" she demanded, incensed, as one hand flattened against her spine and his other hand slid through the silk of her hair.

"Helping you out a little bit," he murmured, his nimble fingers already releasing her hair. He combed his fingers through it deliberately, not stopping the sensual motion until her hopelessly tousled mane fell in soft waves around her face and shoulders. "Much better," he pronounced softly, knowing he was never going to forget the way she looked right here and right now.

Josie shot him a drop-dead look. "I hardly think so."

Wade grinned. There was nothing he enjoyed more than helping a woman realize her full potential. "See for yourself then," he drawled, taking Josie by the shoulders and guiding her toward the mirror. "See?" he goaded cheerfully. He forced her to look at her reflection, noting silently that she looked like a disheveled princess on the lam, just waiting to be captured and tamed by her prince. "You were *made* to wear a dress like this after all."

"No, I wasn't," Josie snapped back stubbornly, defiantly clinging to her tomboy ways. Looking highly insulted by the observation, she twirled around to face him and poked a finger at his chest. "And especially not here. And especially not now."

Wade didn't know why Josie was so opposed to behaving like the sophisticated woman she could so easily be. He did know it was a crying shame to let all that suppressed sensuality and hidden femininity go to waste. A crying shame to let a woman as passionate as Josie ignore her true potential.

"Yes here. Yes now," he countered.

Her glance collided with his. "Oh, what do you know!" Josie sputtered back, incensed.

A lot, Wade thought, as he studied the bright flush of color in Josie's cheeks. He didn't know why he suddenly envisioned the two of them together, locked in a fiery embrace. He just did. And he'd bet—from the sparkle in her azure blue eyes—that Josie was envisioning it, too. Which made his next move one heck of a lot easier.

Half his mouth slanting up in a self-assured grin, he did what he had been wanting to all evening and took her into his arms. Acutely aware of the heavy thudding of his heart, he guided her against him, so they surged against each other, length to length.

"I know this...you're all woman, Josie," he murmured as she studied him with misgiving. "In here." Wade touched her temple gently and felt her tremble softly in response. "And in here." He grazed the silken curve of her breast, just above her heart.

A breathless silence strung out between them. "When are you going to stop fighting it and just let yourself be who and what you were meant to be?" he demanded.

"And what is that?" Josie breathed as he scored his thumb across her lower lip again and again and again.

"Exactly what you think," Wade said, knowing she felt so deliciously warm and right he didn't ever want to let her go. "My woman."

Even as Wade bent his head and kissed her, he knew this one caress wouldn't begin to suffice. Not tonight, or any other. Their lips had just begun to fuse, and already he wanted another kiss that was deeper and more searing and more intimate than the last. Already he wanted another kiss that was full of passion and heat and want and need. And damn her, he thought as she melted against him helplessly, if she didn't seem to want it, too.

* * *

The last thing Josie expected from Wade when he saw her in this dress was a kiss, but as the fiery caress continued, she found herself as lost in the miracle of it as he. She had waited a lifetime to be kissed like this. She had waited a lifetime to feel like this. He tasted so good, so undeniably male. Needing to be closer, she stood on tiptoe and wreathed her arms around him. It felt so good to be wanted. It felt so good to be held against him, Josie thought, as she opened her mouth to the insistent pressure of his. His tongue plundered deep, their kiss taking an even more urgent turn. Her breasts pressed against the solid wall of his chest. She could feel his erection pressing against her, hot and urgent.

Desire welled up inside her. Her knees went weak. Her hips moved. For so long she'd had walls around her heart; she'd wanted nothing more than for someone to tear them down. Now it was happening. Too fast. Way too fast, Josie thought shakily, reminding herself sternly that her relationship with Wade was supposed to be about business and nothing more. Knowing she had to stop it now—if she were to stop it at all—Josie flattened her hands across Wade's chest and shoved with all her might. She tore her lips from his. As they surged apart, as inevitably as they'd come together, Wade stepped back, away from her. He looked stunned by the swift change in her mood.

Aware her lips and body were tingling everywhere they'd touched, Josie rubbed the moisture from her lips and grumbled, "You shouldn't have done that."

Obviously, she thought, as she cast a quick disparaging look at his face, he didn't agree. He thought they should have done that and a whole lot more.

Aware that for the first time in her life she had finally met a man who would give her the complete uncompromising physicality she had always craved, Josie grabbed the discarded elastic band in one hand, the length of her hair in the other, and began quickly redoing her ponytail.

Watching her, Wade merely grinned, "Doesn't matter what hairstyle you're wearing, Josie," he teased, his eyes sparkling with an unabashedly amorous light. "It's not gonna deter me one bit." Just that quickly he hauled her back into his arms and kissed her until she was awash in sensation and moaning low in the back of her throat.

Much more of this, Josie knew, and they'd end up in her bed! She had to do something to cool his ardor. And the only thing she could think of was to ask him what he clearly did not want to be asked. "So," she said breathlessly, breaking free. "Just who is Sandra—" Josie lifted her chin, enunciating clearly "—and what did she do to you?"

"You sure know how to put out the flames."

You sure know how to start them, Josie thought, hoping he would not notice how her knees shook. Josie whirled away from him, her long silk-chiffon skirt rustling as she moved. "Not going to tell me?" Josie prodded mercilessly as she bent to turn on the lights.

Wade scowled as pools of yellow lamplight flooded the trailer living room. He looked very unhappy she'd brought the subject back around to Sandra. Again. Despite the fact he had announced earlier that topic was off-limits to one and all. "Does it look as if I am?" he shot right back, lounging against the counter that separated the kitchen from the living room.

"Okay. Fine. Don't tell me, then." Josie tossed her head like the sassy debutante she once was. "I'll just ask around the next time I'm in Laramie." Satisfied she had successfully cooled Wade's ardor with her nosiness, she said, "I'm sure someone there will know."

He straightened and lazily crossed to her side. "Don't," he advised, wrapping an arm about her waist.

Determined not to let him see how much his nearness was affecting her, Josie lifted an insouciant brow. "Afraid?" she taunted lightly. She wished he would be. Anything to keep her from following her passion and tumbling recklessly into his bed.

His hot gaze skimmed her upturned face as he corrected, "Annoyed."

"Then join the club," Josie advised. Because they had no business kissing each other the way they had. Or ever entertaining kissing each other again. They had a business deal to see to the finish. Getting involved with each other could only interfere with that.

Silence fell between them. Evidently he realized her curiosity about him was as real and long lasting as their kisses had been. He released her, and walked over to examine a houseplant on the counter that had died due to lack of attention some time ago. He rubbed the crumpled brown leaves between his thumb and forefinger. "She was my fiancée," he said at last.

Now they were getting somewhere, Josie thought. "What happened to break the two of you up?" Josie asked. And why was it so hard to discuss?

Wade dropped the crumpled leaves in the dirt that lined the red clay planter. He searched Josie's face for a long moment. "She cheated on me," Wade said grimly. He shrugged his broad shoulders and released a weary sigh. His eyes collided with Josie's again. "And I found out about it in the most humiliating way possible. I came back early from an out-of-town trip and let myself into her apartment and found her in bed with someone else."

Josie could only imagine the horror of that moment. Her heart going out to him, she touched the back of his wrist with her hand. Her eyes holding his, she shook her head and murmured gently, "That must have been awful."

Wade nodded, jaw tightening, and didn't bother to deny it.

Aware his skin was very warm—too warm—Josie dropped her hand and stepped back a pace. "Did Sandra ever give you an explanation why?" It took every ounce of self-restraint Josie possessed to resist the urge to stand on tiptoe and smooth a hand through his hair.

Wade looked as if that had made it even worse. He nodded and reported in a low, matter-of-fact tone. "Sandra said it was clear I cared more about my various investments than I cared about her."

Josie studied him. Along with the hurt was resignation, and some degree of lingering consternation. She knew all about that—the guilt and second-guessing of past events—too, for she had suffered the same. "Did you?" she asked Wade softly. As long as they were being honest.

"Maybe." Wade shoved a hand through his hair. As

he paced the small living room, he flexed his shoulders restlessly. "I don't know." His eyes took on a brooding faraway look. Finally he continued, frustration coloring his low tone. "The hell of it was that Sandra never once told me she felt neglected, let on she was unhappy or gave me a chance to correct things. Instead of telling me how she felt, and why, she ran around behind my back and humiliated me." And that, Josie noted dispassionately as she dumped her long-deceased houseplant in the trash, Wade apparently could not forgive. To the point that he hadn't been serious about a woman since, at least according to Lilah and John McCabe. Since that time he had only dated women they all knew were wrong for him. Josie understood the need to do that, too. It was far easier to wall yourself off from hurt than open yourself up to it once again.

"That must have really hurt," Josie empathized softly.

"It taught me something, though," he said, his low voice firm with resolve. "I'll never be involved with a woman who doesn't trust me enough to confide in me or lies to me again. The first hint of dishonesty, and I am out the door."

The first hint of dishonesty and I am out the door.

His measured words ringing in her ears, Josie felt a flush begin in her chest and creep up her neck. "Why do you date only shallow girls, then—at least according to your parents?"

Wade glanced out the window, at the drilling rig, before returning to her face. "Because at least they're honest with me about what they want from me. Whether it be my money and position or a millionaire cowboy to squire them around, at least I know where I stand with them, and I know why."

That made sense, in a convoluted sort of way, Josie thought, as she took her empty planter over to the sink. "Sandra, I take it, wasn't a debutante, then."

"Nope." Wade leaned against the counter and watched Josie squirt a generous dollop of soap in the planter and then fill it nearly to the brim. "Sandra was the girl next door, the girl everyone loved and trusted. She grew up right here in Laramie County. She was a couple years younger than I was and went to a different high school, so I didn't really get to know her till she'd settled in Houston and began work as an architect there. But once we started dating, as long as we were together, I at least never saw anyone else."

Only, Josie thought, to end up being betrayed. Just as she was betraying him now in a different way. Josie swallowed as guilt assailed her anew. "I've got to get out of this dress," she murmured, her hands clenching the silk. Avoiding his glance, she picked up her long, swirling skirt in both hands and pivoted away from him. "I'll be right back." Her feelings in turmoil, she fled.

So, Wade thought, studying Josie's stricken expression and retreating back. His suspicions were true. Josie was hiding something from him. Gus was obviously struggling mightily with his conscience over something, too. Not to mention the fact that Ernie and Dieter seemed to be looking to Josie for direction, more than giving it to her or simply being on the same Wyatt Drilling Company team. Hell, maybe Ernie and Dieter were hiding something from him, too. The question was what, Wade thought as he began surreptitiously looking around Josie's trailer.

As far as he could tell, everything on the site was proceeding as it would normally. There was nothing unusual about the seismic surveys she had shown him, the samples coming up from the well or the three-dimensional computer exploration. Their integrated expert system had done a superb job of bringing together all the information and processing it. And the heat-flow readings had seemed on the level, too. So what was she hiding? Wade didn't know. But he damn sure intended to find out before all was said and done. And the only way to find out was to stick close to Josie. And to do that, he would need a reason. A damn good one. One she'd be hard-pressed to deny.

Josie emerged from her bedroom, dress box in hand. Though she had a studied air of nonchalance about her, her cheeks were still filled with a guilty flush. And she couldn't quite bring herself to meet his eyes.

Admitting to himself all over again how good Josie looked in the red denim shirt and jeans, Wade snapped his fingers. "I know where—and when—you can wear the dress."

"Really." Josie tossed her mane of glossy dark hair. She gave him a withering look. "Where?"

Wade crossed his arms over his chest. He stood, legs braced apart. "The retirement party for my parents."

Josie blinked. Her tongue snaked out to wet her lower lip. "That's going to be black tie?"

Wade nodded He'd originally intended it to be so, as a way of honoring his parents and a way of giving the good folks of Laramie a chance to kick up their heels and celebrate. Now he had another reason, too. To show off Josie in that dress.

"Wade, I told you," she murmured softly. "I'm not comfortable in clothes like that."

Then she should be, he thought, because she was one beautiful woman—even in jeans. Gussied up, she'd have hearts turning cartwheels all over the place. "Then I'll teach you how to be," he coaxed softly. And maybe in the process he'd get close enough to get her to let down her guard long enough for him to figure out what was really going on here with his land, his money and the hidden lake of oil he was sure was down there somewhere.

Josie licked her lips and continued to stare at him. "You're kidding, right? You're not seriously talking about doing some sort of Pygmalion thing with me?"

He shook his head and stepped as close to her as he dared. "Unless you're afraid it can't be done."

Josie smiled at him tightly and lifted her chin. For a second he thought she was going to try to deck him. "I know it can't be done," she said eventually, regarding him with a hauteur as cold as ice.

Wade grinned back confidently. He ignored the way she had her hands balled into fists and planted on her hips. "You're forgetting. I have the Midas touch."

"And you, cowboy, are forgetting what a tomboy I am at heart."

Wade frowned, his exasperation beginning to get the better of him once again. He ran a hand across his jaw and realized that although he had shaved that morning, he needed another shave. "You're saying I can't do this?"

"I'm saying," Josie corrected evenly, as she elbowed him aside and strode past militantly, "that I won't let you."

Wade shrugged. He watched as she stepped around throw pillows that had tumbled from the sofa to the floor and straightened stacks of business papers that were already perfectly straight. "Fine." He shrugged, aware he hadn't expected her to be this stubborn. Damn it, he liked spending time with her. Even if he wasn't sure he could trust her. And he liked kissing her even more. "Then I can't let Wyatt Drilling keep drilling," he countered, just as mulishly.

Josie was silent.

"That is not fair!"

So what? Wade thought unsympathetically. "Life isn't fair."

Josie stomped away from him, her temper ignited into hot flames of emotion that were glorious to behold. "No wonder you have such a hard time keeping girl-friends," she stormed, "if this is the way you behave!"

Wade had never minded losing any of the shallow society debs he had dated. He hadn't even minded losing Sandra that much, once he had gotten over the shock of her betrayal. He would mind losing Josie. Despite the fact he wasn't sure he could—or should—trust her, he liked having Josie in his life. She made everything seem new and exciting again. He hadn't felt this energized since the first time he'd struck oil on a lease he had acquired in a poker game. Aware she was still watching him carefully, he shrugged laconically. "You want the chance to keep drilling for oil, I get the opportunity to turn you into the lady I know you can be." She'd resist the process all the way of course, which would—in his estimation anyway—make it all the more fun.

Josie narrowed her eyes at him and restlessly tapped one foot. "Why are you really doing this?" she demanded suspiciously.

Wade lifted both hands uncaringly. "Maybe you're right. Maybe I do have a Pygmalion complex. You've already heard how I like to transform the women I date." And maybe he just wanted her to become his woman, at least for a while. One thing was for certain, with Josie Lynn Corbett in his life, the days and nights would never be dull.

"I'm serious, Wade McCabe," Josie persisted in a highly aggravated tone. "Why are you really doing this?"

Easy, Wade thought. "The same reason I do everything," he told Josie with absolute honesty. "The challenge." And he had one heck of a challenge on his hands right now. Their passionate kisses had rocked him as much as they had obviously rocked her. Even now, knowing she was keeping something from him had not deterred his passion for her in the least. In fact, that made him want to take her in his arms and kiss her all over again until she melted against him helplessly, until she surrendered herself to him heart and soul and confessed to him what was really going on here. Unfortunately if he did that, she might not be the only one who lost sight of their end game.

So he was going to have to try another tack to stay

close to her, and this looked like the fastest, easiest way to keep seeing her in as intimate a fashion as possible. Not only would he get to see if his vision of her all gussied up were on the mark, not only would she learn something about holding her own at society shindigs, but if he were right in his suspicions, he would catch her off her guard so he could discover the deception. At the same time he might be able to get her out of his system, figure out why she was all wrong for him, because when he was able to do that—discover her fatal flaw, as it were—that would make his desire for her fade.

On the other hand, Wade mused, if he was wrong, if Josie wasn't out to actively deceive him or betray him in any way, then he'd be making those Cinderella dreams he was sure all girls had come true. Either way, Wade decided, he just couldn't lose.

"He's going to what?" Gus demanded late that evening as he and Josie pored over the latest samples coming out of the well.

Josie brought a steaming pot of coffee over to the table and set it down along with two mugs. She gave Gus a level look. "He's going to teach me how to be a lady." Or at least he was going to try, Josie thought, as she filled two mugs to the brim. There was no way she was going to let him succeed.

Gus shook his head and stirred a generous amount of sugar into his cup. "He's got no idea who he's really dealing with, does he?"

Josie shook her head. She sipped the hot, exceedingly bitter liquid. "None." Yet, anyway, she amended silently. As long as his brother Jackson didn't remember where he'd seen her and put two and two together, Josie's true identity—as a former debutante and Dallas heiress—was safe from being revealed. Because if any of that got out now, before she'd proven her worth as a talented wildcatter in her own right, she'd never be taken seriously. Here or anywhere else, Josie feared. Instead she would be seen as a flighty, irresponsible dilettante who should be kept as far away from other people's money and the wildcatting business as possible.

"Yet you're letting him get away with it, anyway," Gus remarked quietly, amazed. He knew in the past Josie would've died rather than let anyone get the better of her!

Josie shrugged and pushed the memory of Wade McCabe's hot, potent kisses and the ardent way he had been looking at her from her mind. She couldn't afford to get involved with anyone right now, no matter how sensually appealing or masculinely exciting they were.

Josie frowned, very much aware of the way the hunt for oil was dictating her behavior these days. Not necessarily always in a good way. "I don't want to do or say anything that would make Wade want to stop the drilling," she replied tightly, knowing very well just how much was on the line, not just for her, but for Gus, Ernie, Dieter…and Wade, too. "Our situation here is precarious enough as it is. So if my going along with Wade McCabe's ridiculous improvement scheme buys us more time to find oil here, so be it," she declared practically.

Gus studied her, knowing her well enough and long

enough to realize that wasn't the only reason she had given in to Wade's demands. There had to be something more. "What's really in it for you?" the grizzled old roughneck demanded dryly.

The chance of a lifetime, Josie thought, a determined smile curving her lips. Wade McCabe might not know it, but he had pushed one of her own hot buttons with his scheme. She looked up at Gus and vowed in a low, determined voice, "I'm going to teach that way-too-presumptuous, know-it-all cowboy a lesson he'll never forget."

Chapter 5

"As much as I appreciate your willingness to assist us, don't you have your own business to tend to?" Josie asked Wade McCabe politely Tuesday morning. He had been following her around the drilling rig for a good two hours now—to the point he was really underfoot. Worse, it looked as if Wade was really enjoying getting under her skin.

Wade rolled his weight from his heels to his toes, until he was leaning over her, emanating warmth. "Nothing is more important to me right now than this," Wade told her.

"Still," Josie returned smoothly as she paused to check out the vibrating mud screen and the slush pouring into the pit, "if you want to check stock or bond prices or something you can use the phones in our office." Anything to get him out from underfoot.

Wade lifted his Stetson and resituated it squarely on his handsome head. "That's right generous of you to offer," he drawled. But he had no intention of taking her up on her suggestion, Josie saw.

Before she could say anything else, a car pulled up and parked beside the rig. A slender young woman in a tank top, formfitting jeans, straw cowboy hat and boots got out. Seeing her old friend Meg Lockhart, Josie let out a joyous shout and swept heedlessly down the steps. The two women embraced warmly as Wade and the others looked on from above, then Josie drew back. "Are you and your son here for good now?" Josie asked.

Meg nodded. "Jeremy and I got all moved in yesterday, and I start at the hospital later today. But that's not why I'm here." Meg took Josie's hand and drew her out of earshot of the others. "I'm here to deliver a message from your mother."

Josie groaned. "What now?"

"Bitsy wants you to know she is about out of patience. If you aren't back in the city by Friday, working, she's going to take matters into her own hands."

"What's that supposed to mean?" Josie exclaimed, really irritated now. Wasn't it enough her mother had no confidence in her? she thought, incensed. Did she have to keep meddling in her life, too?

"It means I wouldn't put it past her to come down here herself and try to drag you home," Meg replied. "She really wants you back in Dallas. For good, this time. Anyway, I thought you ought to know that she hasn't given up on the idea of you resuming your post at the foundation."

Without warning, a shadow fell over them. Wade

lifted his Stetson and nodded at Meg. "It's been a long time," Wade drawled, smiling at Meg, before taking her in his arms for a warm, welcoming embrace.

Meg hugged Wade back. "Several years, at least," she agreed, looking as pleased to see Wade as he was to see her.

"Couldn't help overhearing," Wade drawled, looking Josie up and down, before finally settling his gaze on her face. "Problem?"

Meg and Josie exchanged looks, with Josie silently beseeching Meg not to say a thing. "My old boss in Dallas wants me back," Josie told Wade, as her heart took on an accelerated beat. "I've already explained I'm not going back, but she won't take no for an answer."

Wade regarded Josie in a lazy, all-male way that made her throat go dry. "That's some transition, isn't it? Going from foundation work to an independent oil company?"

"Oh, I don't know." Josie swept off her hard hat. Using the back of her bare wrist, she wiped the perspiration from her brow. "If you've worked in one office you've worked in them all," Josie muttered cantankerously beneath her breath. It was office work, per se, that she hated. She wanted to be in the outdoors. Climbing around on drilling rigs, or canvasing the land looking for likely drilling spots.

"So, Wade—" Meg changed the subject brightly, coming to Josie's rescue once again "—how are the plans coming for the surprise party in your parents' honor?"

They weren't, Wade thought, but he would get to it shortly, as soon as he took care of this. "Expecting a lot of people to show up on Friday evening?" Meg persisted.

Wade nodded. "The entire hospital staff—past and present—and their spouses. Plus family and friends and various high rollers who have agreed to underwrite the cost of putting beds and equipment in the wing I'm going to build in their honor."

"That's a lot."

Wade nodded, trying not to think about the fact his events planner had quit on him and he had no idea who was going to replace Andrea and make it as glitzy and exciting as he had promised himself the fete for his parents would be. "About five hundred so far, but I'm having to add a few more each day."

Meg crossed her arms in front of her and leaned against the side of her car. "And you've been able to keep it top secret so far?"

Wade shrugged. "They think a society wedding of one of the babies they delivered in the early days is gonna happen there this weekend. And it's black tie. Although it can be hard getting my dad into a tux, it was no problem getting them to agree to attend the nuptials and reception—they love seeing the kids they delivered here when they're all grown-up."

Meg smiled while Josie did her best to fade into the background. Which was unusual behavior on her part, to say the least. "That's great," Meg said.

"You're coming, too, aren't you?" Wade asked Meg, knowing it wouldn't be a party unless all four Lockhart sisters showed up.

Meg slanted Josie another sidelong glance and

nodded. "Wouldn't miss it for the world," Meg told Wade warmly.

"So how is it you two know each other?" Wade asked, looking first at Josie, who seemed increasingly uneasy having Meg and Wade anywhere near each other, then at Meg. "Did you go to college together?" Wade asked Meg bluntly.

Meg tensed. Abruptly she seemed at a complete loss for words. Color flooded her cheeks. "No, um—"

"Actually," Josie interrupted swiftly, sending Meg another follow-my-lead look.

Meg got Josie's silent message and backed up. "I'd love to stay and chat but I've got my five-year-old son, Jeremy, waiting for me at Jenna's dress shop. We're having lunch together before I head to work." With a merry little wave, she got in her car, slammed the door, and drove off.

"Funny, she didn't answer my question," Wade said, when the dust had cleared. More sure than ever that Josie—and everyone close to her—was hiding something from him, Wade regarded Josie steadily. "So, how did the two of you meet?"

"A mutual friend introduced us years ago," Josie said truthfully, though that friend had been her mother.

Wade's eyes took on a cynical glint. "Where?"

In the Corbett Foundation offices, when Meg had come to interview for a nursing school scholarship and Bitsy had asked Josie to sit in. Not only had Meg won it over all the candidates, hands down, Meg and Josie had become fast friends. But Josie didn't want to tell Wade that, because if she did he'd quickly realize not only that she was one of the Dallas Corbetts and an heiress to boot in her own right, but he might very well remember the old scandal and figure out who her father was, too.

Josie frowned, making no effort at all to mask her annoyance with his persistent questioning. "What is this?" she said with a levity she couldn't begin to feel as the two of them squared off under the increasingly hot Texas sun. "The third degree?"

He shrugged, his powerful shoulders straining against the damp cotton fabric of his shirt. "Just curious. I've known Meg a long time. We grew up together. And prior to this the only issue I've ever known her to dodge is—"

"Her son, Jeremy, and who his father is," Josie supplied quickly.

"You do know her," Wade said, impressed, while Josie headed for the nearest spot of shade on the side of one of the trailers.

Josie drew a deep breath. She knew that was a secret Meg might very well take to her grave. "The way I see it, that's her business," Josie retorted calmly. Hers and Jeremy's. Aware Wade was still watching her far too closely for comfort, Josie decided this was as good a time as any to make a point. She stuck her hands in the pockets of her jeans, rocked back and dug the heels of her boots into the dirt. "I don't ask questions when none are welcomed."

Wade regarded her with a smug, knowing look. "You hinting for me to back off?"

Josie shrugged. "If the boot fits."

Not waiting for him to reply—or heaven forbid ask

any more nosy questions—Josie marched off. Once back on the drilling rig platform, she was immediately bombarded with questions from Ernie and Dieter. Josie knew exactly what to do. She started to answer, then— catching sight of Wade—thought better of looking like a know-it-all and called Gus over to confer with them, as well.

"Mind if I hear this, too?" Wade asked casually.

What could Josie say to that? It was his land they were standing on, his discovery well they were drilling.

Josie nodded, swallowing around the unaccustomed tightness in her throat. Ignoring Wade as much as possible, she continued discussing the problem they were having with the drilling mud, and how they might adjust the consistency of it for better results.

By the time they had finished their discussion, some thirty minutes later, and decided on a plan of action, it was very clear to Wade that Josie was as knowledge-able as the three men, and exceedingly practical about the overall financial considerations to boot. He noted with relief that if she had anything to say about what was going on at the site—and she apparently had a lot of input—his discovery well was in good hands.

Gus looked at Josie as the discussion wrapped up. "Me and the boys'll get on it right away," he promised.

Josie nodded, looking every bit as satisfied as Wade felt with the plan of action they had concocted. "And I'll take this latest data back to the trailer and enter it into the computers," she said.

More curious than ever about the undeniably beauti-ful tomboy calling the shots, Wade followed her into the trailer. "What is your title again?" Wade asked as Josie sat down at the computer and switched it on. She was pretending to be an entry-level member of the team, but it was clear that her crew was looking to her for direction every bit as much as they were looking to the much more experienced Gus. Which was unusual to say the least, Wade thought.

"Good question." Josie shrugged as she booted up the computer. "Normally, I'd be an administrative assistant or all-round gal Friday to Big Jim. Only he wouldn't let me go to South America with him and his crew—"

"That annoyed you, didn't it?" Wade interrupted, aware from the look on her face that he'd struck a nerve. "That he wouldn't let you go."

Josie scowled, her frustration with the situation apparent. "He said it was no place for a woman."

"But you disagreed."

Josie opened the file that dealt with drilling mud viscosity and began entering data with a vengeance, her fingers speeding over the keys. "I think I could have managed there just fine." Her back went rigid and her soft lips clamped together in a stubborn line. "It might have been my first time on a site out of the country or in the jungle, but it wasn't my first time on a site."

And yet, Wade knew, about that much Big Jim may have had a point. "Can't say I blame him for wanting to protect you," Wade offered.

Josie shot him a withering look. Clearly, she did not appreciate him siding with Big Jim. "It was chauvinism, plain and simple," Josie disagreed bluntly. "But I'm doing fine here, anyway." She saved her document and switched over to the file recording drilling depths. "I'm just filling in and helping out the rest of the operation—what little of it is left here anyway—as I'm needed in Big Jim's absence."

Wade glanced down at Josie's notes. "Who's in the office in Odessa now?"

"No one." Finished, Josie swiftly switched over to yet another file, typing in current weather conditions and how those related to the drilling that had been done that week. "All the calls are being automatically forwarded to the site here."

That sounded good, except for the fact Wade had a feeling she had totally usurped Big Jim's authority. What puzzled him was that Gus, who'd been with Big Jim on one job or another almost since the beginning of Big Jim Wyatt's wildcatting operation, was going along with it. And Wade had to ask himself why. Wade wondered if something had happened to Big Jim. Was it possible Big Jim had been incapacitated in some way down in South America—or even before the majority of Jim's regular crew headed off down there to work? If so, why wouldn't they just say so?

Were they afraid Wade would take his drilling contract to another independent? 'Cause the truth was, without Big Jim here to run things personally, now or at any point in the future, he just might. Any independent operation was only as good as the wildcatter in charge. And generally speaking, Big Jim was worth waiting around for, he was so good at finding oil.

Wade looked at Josie, who was still typing away vigorously. Instinct told him that Josie was at the center of whatever was going on here. To uncover the deception—and he was more certain than ever there was some deception going on here—he was going to have to get close to her.

Figuring there was no time like the present to accomplish that, he perched on the edge of her desk and cut straight to the chase. "Where did you go to school?"

Josie kept typing and refused to meet his eyes. "In Austin, at the University of Texas."

Wade had the sudden impression he wasn't just being held at arm's length. He was being pushed away. For good. The thought was damn disturbing. And yet here he was, following her around like a lost puppy. What kind of spell had she put on him? And why was it so important he figure her out, anyway? When he could have very easily just said to heck with it, closed the whole drilling operation down and walked away. It wasn't like him to want anything to do with someone he was fairly sure was deceiving him.

"What did you major in?" His voice was soft, conciliatory.

Her reaction was not. She seemed to get even further away from him emotionally as she recited in a low, battle-weary voice, "I received a liberal arts degree, with a concentration in humanities. But," she added almost defiantly as she punched save, "I took as many geology classes as I could fit into my schedule."

It was easy to see she had a chip on her shoulder when it came to her latest job choice. And there was absolutely no reason for it as far as he could see. "Why not just major in geology, geophysics or petroleum engineering if you were interested in this as a career?" Wade asked curiously.

Josie's soft, bare lips twisted wryly. "It would have been the smart thing to do, wouldn't it?"

Frustrated she was not more talkative, Wade clasped his hands loosely between his spread thighs and leaned forward. "So why didn't you?"

Josie uncapped the bottle of spring water on her desk and drank deeply from it. Her eyes lasered into his. "Because at the time I was more interested in finding my Mr. Right, getting married and settling down and having a family of my own. And I didn't think a career as a wildcatter was compatible with that," she said matter-of-factly, not at all shy about admitting her previous, highly romantic dreams. "So I took a job in a Dallas high-rise, and met all manner of eligible men."

Wade didn't want to think of her in anyone's arms but his. Any more than he wanted to think of her being unhappy. "What happened?" he asked softly.

Josie tugged her T-shirt and wiped off the rim of the bottle with the hem of her shirt. "Five years passed. I didn't find the man of my dreams, and was no closer to having the big happy family I've always wanted." Shrugging, she offered him the bottle. As he took it, their hands brushed lightly.

In the soft morning light of the trailer office, her classically beautiful features—high, sculpted cheeks, full lips and wide deep-set eyes—were more pronounced. In deference to the hard hat she'd been wearing earlier, her glossy dark brown hair was caught in a low ponytail at the nape of her neck. But wispy tendrils escaped to frame her face.

Josie watched as he lifted the bottle and placed his lips where hers had been only moments before. "I decided it was dumb for me to wait around for Prince Charming to come and sweep me off my feet," she continued as he drank deeply of the cool spring water.

Josie picked up a pencil off her desk and tapped it restlessly against the stack of papers in front of her. "Now I realize it's up to me to make my dreams come true. And if I don't do that," she said firmly, "if I don't take the risks and follow through—I've got no one to blame but myself."

"Ever think about going back and getting a degree in petroleum engineering—if you're so interested in this?" Wade asked curiously. He was beginning to see she'd make a damn fine oil woman someday. Heck, she might even be talented enough and knowledgeable enough to go out on her own. Especially if they struck oil here and she added that to her résumé, he thought.

Josie frowned. For the first time that day her eyes took on a troubled glimmer. "I've got to try out the lifestyle first, figure out if I am as good at this—at drilling discovery wells—as I think I'm gonna be," she said softly.

Finished, Josie switched off her computer. "I'm going to get an apple. You want one?"

Wade shook his head. "Not right now, thanks."

Wade's gut told him there was still a lot she was holding back—a lot he'd be wise to be concerned about here. Aware Josie was still watching him closely as she stood and moved away from her desk, Wade glanced around him at the office.

Odds were there was an answer or two in the trailer, if only he had the time and opportunity to go through it without Josie knowing. Considering how much money was at stake, he figured he was well within his rights to get those answers—and uncover any deceptions—any way he could.

"Is that offer to use your office still good?" he asked casually. "'Cause I've got something I could fax to my office back in Houston. And a few phone calls to make about the party for my folks."

"No problem," Josie said, looking relieved. "I'll go get that apple. And maybe check on the guys, see how they're doing, while I'm at it."

To Wade's frustration, a quick look around the on-site office netted little more than his cursory search of the trailer where Josie was sleeping the night before. Nothing but a lot of papers bearing the J. L. Wyatt signature. There were also a lot of notes and records—all in Josie's much-neater, more-feminine handwriting. That could have meant everything, had she been the one giving the orders, Wade knew.

Or nothing, if all she were doing was simply recording what was going on so Big Jim could go over it later.

To Wade's frustration, there was nothing that hinted at any sort of fraud going on. Nothing to indicate the operation was anything but aboveboard, except for Big Jim's absence.

And that was peculiar. Wade had never known Big Jim to leave one job for another the whole time he had hired Big Jim Wyatt to drill wildcat wells on any of his various properties.

Then again, Wade couldn't recall Big Jim ever having the opportunity to take his whole crew and "consult" on what could possibly be a major find in the South American jungle, either.

Big Jim had probably felt the well was in capable hands when he'd left it to Gus and Josie and the others. And if they hit oil shortly, as everyone here was hoping and predicting, then Wade had nothing to complain about.

Meanwhile, he had Josie Lynn Corbett to contend with. The first woman ever to work for Big Jim, in any capacity, she was a handful all right: cute in her pink hard hat, and a regular know-it-all when it came to computers, all sorts of geographical data and record keeping. She was a smooth-as-silk negotiator, too: she had talked him into keeping the drill going when he'd been determined to shut it down.

No wonder Big Jim had capitulated and given her a job, despite her sex and minimal qualifications. She not only appeared to have a love for the business in general, but she was also good at dealing with people.

Especially land owners like him. And the guys on the team listened to her, too.

"Find what you were looking for?" Josie said coolly.

Wade grimaced. He'd been so caught up in his thoughts he hadn't heard her come in. He continued searching the open drawer in front of him. "I was looking for a pen." Among other things.

Josie strode forward, half-eaten apple in hand. "There are half a dozen of them right in front of you."

"So there are."

She pressed her lips together mutinously. "What was it you wanted to fax?"

"I, uh, hadn't typed it up yet."

"I see," she said tightly.

Wade stood and reached for his Stetson. "Actually, now that I think about it, maybe I should just use my own computer back at the ranch house." It hadn't taken him long to figure out this spy business was not for him.

"Maybe you should." Her voice dropped another icy notch.

Wade shoved a hand through his hair and settled his hat on his head. He hated the thought he had hurt her feelings. "Any word today from Big Jim?" he asked curiously.

"None." Josie took a big bite of apple. Her expression was as distracted as it was furious. "As I told you, there are no phone lines, no cell phone towers, nothing at the site." She suddenly pitched her apple core in the trash and strode toward him, wiping her hands down the sides of her jeans as she went. "Now, tell me what you were really doing just now. And give me the truth."

Wade knew how he'd like an argument like this to end—in bed. But given the fact they still barely knew each other, that was not likely to happen. "I was snooping," he said calmly.

"Into our operation?"

Wade regarded Josie steadily, realizing he wanted to know a heck of a lot more about Josie Lynn Corbett than that. And he had all along. "Into your private life."

That, she hadn't expected. Josie swallowed, aware Wade McCabe had kept her feeling off guard since the moment he had walked onto the site, and given the exceedingly unpredictable way things were going that wasn't likely to change.

"My private life!" she echoed, astonished.

"I wondered." Determined to keep her off her guard, Wade blurted out the first—and perhaps most important—question that came to mind, "Are you seeing anyone special right now?"

Josie lifted a brow. "You're telling me it makes a difference to you one way or another if I have a boyfriend," she reiterated dryly.

"I don't go around kissing women who are betrothed or otherwise hitched up to someone else."

Josie sighed and tried to look sympathetic to his plight. "I guess, considering what happened to you and Sandra, you wouldn't."

"No," Wade agreed. "I wouldn't." He paused. "So is there someone?" Wade asked persistently.

Josie swallowed. "No."

"Has there ever been?"

"Yes." Josie averted her gaze. "A very long time ago. But I don't want to talk about that. So, if you don't mind," she said archly, "I think you've been underfoot enough."

He tipped his hat at her and headed for the door. "For the time being, I guess you're right. I've got a lot of work to do regarding the party on Friday in any case."

"I imagine you do," Josie retorted dryly, feeling both relieved and disappointed.

"But I'll be back tonight," he promised.

"Tonight? Why?"

Wade winked. "For that dancing lesson I owe you," he said.

* * *

"Didn't think I was serious about this, did you?" Wade drawled some six hours later as he breezed into her trailer and set down the portable stereo and stack of compact discs he'd brought with him.

Josie's pretty eyes widened with amazement. "Not in this lifetime, no," she murmured, agitated.

Wade struggled to keep his matter-of-fact mood. It wasn't easy. Josie had recently showered and changed into white jeans and a blue T-shirt that hugged her slender but curvy frame with disturbing accuracy. Her hair was damp and clean and scented faintly with a floral shampoo. Her face bore the golden glow of the sun, her lips the soft clear sheen of gloss.

"Let's get started," Wade said.

Her eyes glinting stubbornly, Josie shook her head. "I've got core samples to study tonight," she said.

Investment or no, Wade knew she had already worked hard enough for one day. He bent to plug in his stereo. "That can wait till tomorrow," he told her easily. "You've got to get ready for Friday night."

"I agreed to the lessons," Josie reminded.

And only, Wade thought, to prove him wrong—to prove that she was not capable of being turned into the grand Texas lady he felt she could be, if she only put forth some effort.

"I did not agree to be your date Friday night," Josie continued in righteous indignation.

Wade plucked a disc from its cover and slid it into the stereo. He thought he knew where her emotion was coming from. "There's no reason to be afraid," he soothed, all too aware he at least had been waiting for this moment all day.

"I'm not afraid," Josie shot back with a toss of her head.

"You're gonna do fine," Wade continued confidently.

Unfortunately she didn't do fine. Her steps were awkward and awful. And she looked down her nose at him even as she trembled in his arms. "See?" Her mouth twisting in frustration, Josie stepped on his toes and pushed away. "I told you I was no good at this."

He caught her wrist with his free hand before she could escape and anchored her implacably at his side. "You're not trying," he said softly. But she would—before the night was over.

Suddenly Josie was having trouble drawing air into her lungs. "You don't have a clue how hard I'm concentrating," she murmured back, suddenly looking genuinely distressed.

Wade had never met a woman who had so little grasp of the beat of music, Wade admitted reluctantly to himself. Was it possible, he wondered, that she really was every bit as bad at dancing as she seemed? That just like when it came to anything else remotely domestic or feminine, Josie really had no clue?

If so, would it be possible to teach her?

Then again, he thought confidently, his Midas touch had never failed him yet.

"Hang on." He let her go as swiftly as he had claimed her. More determined than ever to help her be all the woman she could be, he vowed, "I'll find us another song."

* * *

Her arms folded defiantly in front of her, Josie watched Wade punch a button. Seconds later the soft sounds of Garth Brooks singing "To Make You Feel My Love" filled the beat-up trailer. Wade turned it up slightly and came back to her.

Josie was annoyed to find herself flushing warmly from head to toe again. She told herself it was the way he filled up the space in the small trailer or the deeply romantic nature of the ballad that caused her to react that way. It had nothing to do with him and the way he had kissed her the other night. The way he wanted to kiss her again, judging from the ardent light in his eyes.

"You don't have to look so hesitant," he said against her hair as the nearness of him and the slow, breathless intimacy of the song filled her senses to overflowing. "I'm not going to step on your toes." Then he took her resisting body in his arms.

But I might step on yours, Josie thought, as she breathed in the deliciously clean and brisk scent of sandalwood and leather clinging to his skin. "I'm not hesitant. I'm annoyed," Josie explained, doing her best to keep her dance steps falling between the beats instead of directly on the beats. Which was, as it happened, a lot harder than she thought it would be.

Wade met her gaze affably and gave her another coaxing grin. "Annoyed about what?" he prodded softly, tugging her close and kissing the top of her ear.

Josie told herself sternly she was not enjoying being held in Wade's arms. Nor was she enjoying the feel of his lips ghosting over her skin. "Having to dance on command---with anyone," she said.

Wade drew back, to better study her face. "Most women I know like to dance."

Maybe they haven't done enough of it with partners they care very little for, Josie thought, trying not to notice how he had splayed his hand across the middle of her back in a proprietary way.

Deciding he was having a little bit too much fun with this—and the same thing could happen to her if she didn't clamp down on the unmistakable chemistry flowing between them—Josie lurched into him with comical awkwardness. Then, for good measure, accidentally-on-purpose tromped on his foot. "Whoops," she said, lurching into him again.

Wade grimaced as her knee thudded against his shin, but retained his light, possessive grip on her. "No problem," he said, grunting as Josie elbowed him in the chest. "So how come you don't like to dance?" Wade persisted, as they lumbered on, their steps completely out of sync.

Maybe, Josie thought, because she had never danced with him. Because even with her doing her best to keep stumbling and moving in klutzy counterpoint to the beat, it was still enjoyable being held gallantly in his embrace. Every bit as enjoyable, in fact, as it had been kissing him. "I'm just not good at it," Josie fibbed.

Wade quirked his brow. "You just haven't had enough practice," he disagreed.

Little did he know! If she was ever again closeted up in another stuffy ballroom it would be too soon, Josie thought. "Face it," Josie said, as Garth Brooks's voice faded and Trisha Yearwood's voice came on. "Some women are just not cut out for fancy events and fancy dresses and fancy-women-lovin' men."

Wade's eyes darkened to a deeper brown. "Is that what you think I am? A fancy-woman-lovin' man?"

Josie flushed and dropped her gaze to the muscled contours of his chest. "You know what I mean."

"No," he said emphatically. "I don't. Explain it to me."

Josie drew a deep breath. It upset her to bring all this up, but she knew it had to be said. Wade had to start facing the fact they were and always would be all wrong for each other.

"The kind of man who wants his woman all gussied up and waiting for him at the end of a long day whether he actually comes home or not. The kind of man who spends his life gallivanting all over Texas, chasing down one oil deal after another and doing exactly what he pleases while his woman waits patiently for him at home."

Wade quirked a brow. To her chagrin, he looked more interested than upset. "Sounds as if you don't like waiting at home," he drawled as the second song ended and a third began.

Josie thrust her chin out stubbornly. "I'm not the waiting-patiently-in-the-background type," she said flatly as Wade matched his steps to the up-tempo beat.

Wade slid his hand down her spine, not stopping until it rested just below her waist. "Well, you'll be happy to know that if—and when—I ever do decide to settle down with just one woman, that I plan on being with her every second I can," he vowed determinedly, his ardent gaze roving her upturned face. "No matter what dreams I'm chasing down."

"What about her dreams?" Josie persisted, taking his hand and moving it back up to mid-spine.

"She can have those, too," he promised, his grin widening merrily. "In fact—" Wade paused long enough to tap the end of Josie's nose with his forefinger "—I'll make sure I do everything possible to make sure my woman gets what she wants out of life, in terms of her own career, too."

Josie rolled her eyes. Wade was making this out to be easy when it wasn't. "It sounds good in theory."

Wade's eyes darkened unhappily. "But you don't really see it happening," Wade guessed.

Josie lifted her slender shoulders as the third song ended and a lively two-step began. "Forgive me for being skeptical—"

"But bitter experience has taught you otherwise?"

Irritated he saw so much of her feelings when she wanted him to see so little, Josie admitted grimly, "I was engaged once. When I finally got up the courage to tell Ben what I really wanted to do with my life—spend it finding and digging wildcat oil wells—you know what he did? He laughed. And told me to forget it. No wife of his was ever going to be a lady roughneck." Josie's heart ached as she recalled the hurt and humiliation she'd felt to find out that Ben didn't have faith in her, either. Never had and never would.

"I'm sorry." Wade's eyes filled with compassion. His hold on her gentled even more.

"So was I," Josie shot back adamantly, trying hard not to succumb to the tenderness she saw in Wade's eyes. "So sorry that I ended the engagement then and there."

Wade gave her a considering look. "I don't blame you."

Josie hesitated. "You don't?" Of all the people who knew about the situation, Wade was the first to support her view.

He shook his head. "You deserve the full backing and unceasing encouragement of the man in your life, whatever your dreams."

Josie studied him, taking in the rumpled windswept layers of his ash brown hair and handsome suntanned face. "You really believe that?" she whispered, amazed, as her heart began a slow, fluttering beat.

"You bet your bottom dollar I do," Wade countered firmly as yet another song began.

Emotions awhirl, Josie tightened her grip on Wade. She looked into his eyes. "It seems I've misjudged you," she murmured apologetically.

"No problem," Wade retorted easily. "I can forgive you for being skeptical."

Josie tightened her grip on him and breathed a sigh of relief.

Wade continued sternly, "What I can't forgive is the fibbing you did—"

At the censure in his low voice, Josie froze. "What?"

Wade flashed her a crocodile smile as his hot gaze raked her from head to toe. He stopped dancing, too. "Honey, you've been two-stepping like there's no to-morrow for five minutes now, and your steps are smooth as silk. The only way you could do that so well and so easily is if you already knew how to dance."

Strong arm cinching her waist, he hauled her against him, hip to hip, and thigh to thigh. "Admit it," he growled.

She took exception to his flat, insistent tone.

"When it comes to dance floor expertise, you've got more than your share, and—pleasurable as it's been holding you in my arms," Wade said, face hardening, "it's not due to anything I've taught you."

Loathing the fact she'd been caught in a cleverly laid trap, Josie flushed from head to toe and pushed away from Wade. She drew herself up straighter, so the top of her head almost reached his chin. "I admit pulling your leg about the dancing in order to discourage you, but not about the rest," she told him with a haughty toss of her head. "I'm not the kind of woman who wants to spend a big part of her life wearing evening gowns and pearls. And I never will be." And whether Wade admitted it to himself or not, that was the kind of wife a millionaire Texan like Wade needed. He needed someone like Josie's mother, Bitsy, who adored living the high life and flitting from one gala event to another. Not someone like Josie who preferred to spend the rest of her life in jeans and a hard hat.

Wade regarded Josie skeptically. He released a long breath and jammed his hands on his waist. The action pushed back the edges of his mocha suede sport coat, revealing the flatness of his abdomen beneath the starched white crispness of his shirt and his faded, black Levi's jeans. "You haven't given that kind of life a chance," he told her brashly.

If only he knew, Josie thought miserably, recalling

how she'd been torn between the two worlds in which she'd lived for as long as she could remember, and now wanted to find her own niche where she could be appreciated for who and what she was, not denigrated for what she was not. A place where she could be comfortable just being herself no matter what.

"But that's about to change," Wade promised as he flattened a hand against her spine and tugged her closer. He lowered his head swiftly and delivered a sexy kiss. As his lips caressed hers lightly, evocatively at first, then with growing ardor, Josie could almost believe everything would be different in her life if only she were dating him. But common sense told her not to put too much stock in any man, particularly if said attraction got in the way of her dreams.

And right now, Josie reminded herself firmly, as she felt her traitorous body melting helplessly into his, she was here in Laramie County, Texas, for one reason and only one reason: to make a reputation that would earn her the respect she craved.

Her goals reaffirmed and clearly defined, she put both hands on Wade's chest and pushed away from him. "Dancing lesson or no, don't think you can transform me into what you want me to be or need me to be, because you can't," Josie warned, still trembling from the sexy kiss. Her parents had tried that, to disastrous result! The resulting unhappiness had torn them apart and made what had always been a difficult situation even worse!

Wade saw her response and grinned in satisfaction. "Change can be good," he reminded softly, looking like he wanted to haul her close and kiss her all over again.

"Not," Josie said right back, ignoring the flutter of desire deep inside her as she stomped over to shut off the soft romantic music, "when it's forced on you by someone else." Just so he wouldn't miss her point, she made a great show of unplugging his stereo and handing it back to him. She swept him, head to toe, with a deeply disparaging look. "Time to say good-night and be on your way, cowboy."

Unfortunately the offense she had hoped he would take at her blatant lack of hospitality did not materialize. Instead Wade McCabe only looked all the more determined to make her his.

"I'll be back," Wade promised, his brown eyes twinkling merrily.

Her emotions in turmoil, Josie sighed. How well she knew that.

Chapter 6

"She's afraid of intimacy," Wade declared an hour later. "That's why she won't go to the party with me Friday night."

Shane, his younger brother, who was busy scouting for a likely place to set up his own horse ranch and had decided to crash at Wade's ranch house for the night rather than endure any more of his mother's infernal matchmaking, grinned and slapped him on the back. "You just keep telling yourself that, Brother," he counseled with a knowing wink, "and maybe you'll believe it."

"I know what I'm talking about," Wade insisted stubbornly. He knew because it was an emotion he'd often felt himself. If you let yourself be vulnerable to another human being, you opened yourself up to the possibility that other person could hurt you. Josie didn't want to be hurt any more than he did. But he wasn't going to hurt her. His desire was to help her, to give her the inner confidence she needed to be all the woman she could be, because confidence was one thing he not only understood, but had in abundance of, in both his work and his social life.

"Otherwise, why would she make such a big deal over a simple kiss?" Or two or three? Or the dozen more and then some he'd like to give her.

Shane narrowed his eyes at Wade. "The question is, why would you?"

Wade brushed off his baby brother's concern. There was nothing out of the ordinary about his desire for Josie. She had caught his eye. It was natural for him to pursue the attraction. "I'm fine," he said. More than fine.

Shane rolled his eyes. "Sure you are."

Wade scowled. "I am!"

Shane lifted a skeptical brow. "And that's why you've been talking about nothing but kissing Josie Lynn Corbett for the past half hour."

Wade made a face. "Her reaction to it—" *to me,* he added silently "—puzzles me, that's all."

"Uh-huh. You've kissed a lot of women in your time, Wade, and I imagine more than one of 'em has had a reaction that was less than 100 percent favorable, yet I never heard you grumbling about any of them kicking you out of their place immediately after el smackeroo."

That's because he had never cared in quite this way before. Wade rubbed the late-night stubble on his jaw and stared out at the starry Texas night. A much-needed rain was predicted for morning, but so far there was no sign of it. "Maybe you're right. Maybe this is different," he said finally as he stuck a package of popcorn in the microwave.

Shane opened a long-necked bottle of Lone Star beer and drank deeply. "How so?"

Wade watched the paper bag in the microwave slowly begin to inflate. "Because I don't trust her and I'm still attracted to her." Since Sandra had betrayed him that had not been the case. Trust was the big litmus test with every and any woman he dated. One hint of dishonesty and he was out of there. Yet with Josie he kept going back.

Shane frowned as the popcorn began to pop and the buttery smell filled the room. He reached into the refrigerator and handed Wade a beer. "That's the kind of woman you want to stay away from."

Wade got out two bowls. "Tell me about it."

"So why don't you?" Shane asked as the microwave timer dinged and the oven shut off.

Wade opened the door. Being careful not to burn himself, he lifted the bag out by the edges. "Because she's working at the site where they're drilling my discovery well, that's why."

Wade opened the bag then stood back as a wealth of fragrant, buttery steam escaped.

"You could fire her," Shane said, as Wade divided the popcorn equally into two bowls. "Tell her to go back to Odessa."

Wade shook his head as he took a sip of beer, then popped a few hot, fluffy kernels of corn into his mouth. "Nope. I want her here. But you're right. I do need to take action, to get control of the situation," Wade said firmly. And now that he thought about it, he knew exactly what to do.

The ringing of the phone brought Josie out of a sound sleep. Groaning, she rolled over, grabbed the receiver and put it to her ear. A glance at the clock told her it was one in the morning.

"Josie Lynn!" Her father's familiar voice floated over the telephone wires. "I'm glad I caught you, hon."

Josie struggled to hear above the sound of the rain pounding on the roof of her trailer. She sat up against the headboard. She'd forgotten to adjust the thermostat before she went to bed. It was obvious the air conditioner was working overtime. She shivered in the cool air and dragged the sheet up across her breasts.

"I didn't think you could get to a phone."

"The oil company flew me back in a chopper to the closest town," Big Jim explained in his boisterous voice.

Knowing it must be important if her dad went to this much trouble to call her, Josie reached over and switched on a light.

"Great news, hon. We struck oil and it's a huge field. They want me and the men to stay on and continue drilling their discovery wells. Which, considering the size of the lake we're sitting on, means I'll be here for at least six months or longer."

At the pure excitement in her dad's voice, Josie's heart sank. She could continue this ruse a little while longer. But indefinitely…? she thought, as the rain picked up intensity outside. Someone would be sure to catch on. And that someone was likely to be Wade McCabe.

"So I think the best thing for you to do," Big Jim continued, "is go back to Dallas and be with your mama and work at the Corbett Foundation again."

Josie swallowed.

News of a huge new South American oil field—and the wildcatter who'd been successful in drilling down to it—wouldn't stay quiet for long. Unless he were so busy and diverted he was entirely cut off from the news in the oil world, Wade McCabe would be sure to hear about it.

Which in turn would mean he'd also learn Big Jim Wyatt had no intention of coming back to Texas anytime soon. Wade would then want to talk to Big Jim, and once he did— Oh, mercy, Josie thought. Mercy!

Guilt cascading over her in near-paralyzing waves, Josie buried her face in her hands, as a childhood saying came back to haunt her with amazing speed. "When first we practice to deceive, what a tangled web we weave." She'd done that all right and then some, Josie admitted to herself miserably.

"And that will make your mama so happy," Big Jim continued. "To have you back in the city, where you belong."

But that was the problem, Josie thought. She didn't belong in the city. Never had. She belonged out in the Texas countryside, where she could combine the passion of looking for oil and the science of finding it into a family tradition of her very own. "I can't do that, Dad." Completely energized and wide awake, Josie leaped determinedly from her bed. She'd come too far to give up now.

"Sure you can," Big Jim disagreed.

Josie shoved the hair from her face as she padded barefoot, wearing nothing but a T-shirt and panties, out to the small trailer kitchen to make some coffee.

"Okay, then let me rephrase," Josie told her dad tightly, not caring what this call from halfway around the world was costing as long as they got this much straight. "I don't want to do that."

Big Jim blew out an exasperated breath. "Now, Josie, be reasonable. There's not a darn thing for you to do there in Odessa except tell people me and my men are out of the country, and Gus can do that as well as you."

Now was the time to tell him the truth—that she wasn't in Odessa—that his call had simply been electronically forwarded to her here.

It was time to tell Big Jim she had taken a giant gamble—and accepted a job on his behalf she'd had no business and no authority to accept—and just be done with it, Josie lectured herself sternly.

And yet she couldn't. Because if she did, she knew exactly what her dad would do. He'd get Wade on the phone, now, even if it was the middle of the night, and that would be the end of her wildcatting days, period.

And Josie couldn't give up now. Not when she was so close to achieving everything she had ever dreamed of. Not when she was so close to making her parents proud.

Pushing her considerable pangs of conscience aside, Josie blew out an exasperated breath of her own and tried to prepare her dad, well in advance, for the inevitable truth telling.

"I told you I wanted to be involved in the business—" *And if you had just let me. If you'd just be-*

lieved in me, or tried to include me or given me a chance, I wouldn't have had to take such drastic measures.

"And I let you fool around a bit in the office so you could feel a part of things," Big Jim continued in the patronizing tone Josie hated, "but by now you must see that wildcatting isn't the life for you."

What wildcatting? Josie fumed. All her dad had "allowed" her to do was answer the phones and take messages! This after dragging her to countless sites all over Texas, and some even in the Gulf of Mexico, and teaching her from the ground up just what exactly it was he did for a living.

Had he not kept her so close to his side during her court-ordered visitations with him, had he not taught her everything he knew about the oil-finding business, Josie might never have known how much she loved it.

But he had and she did, and now they were both going to have to find a way to deal with that.

Josie filled the reservoir with water, hunted for a clean spoon and stuffed a paper napkin in the bottom of the plastic cone over the drip hole and dumped in what she thought was the right amount of coffee grounds.

"You're wrong, Dad," Josie told Big Jim bluntly as she switched on the coffeemaker and looked out her kitchen window at the drilling rig in the distance. "This is the life for me." Josie frowned as she saw the flashlights arcing and three men running back and forth on the drilling platform. "And I'll prove it to you, Daddy."

Perdition! Something was wrong! It had to be if they were all up in the middle of the night! Scowling and mentally swearing at this continued run of bad luck they were having on the drilling site, Josie pivoted on her heel and headed for her bedroom, the portable phone still pressed to her ear. Snatching the closest pair of mud-and grease-streaked jeans from the pile of laundry on the floor, Josie cradled the phone between her shoulder and ear. She perched on the edge of her bed and struggled into them.

"No, honey, you won't," Big Jim stated in his firmest tone of voice while Josie rolled her eyes and searched around for a work shirt to put on over her fire-engine-red Roughnecks Do It Better T-shirt. "Now you go on back to Dallas like your mama wants. Because she is right about this, you'll see. And then I'll see you when I get home."

Before Josie could get another word in edgewise, the line went dead.

With an oath Josie yanked the receiver away from her ear and made a face at the phone. Leave it to her father to continue to insist on having the last word, while depriving her of the chance to speak her mind to him! But there was no time to worry about that or the fact that her father hadn't even asked her what she'd been up to.

Instead, Josie thought, as she scrambled around for her beat-up red cowgirl boots and shoved her feet into them, Big Jim had just assumed she'd been sitting around twiddling her thumbs, awaiting his return!

Thinking back on it, Josie didn't know why she was surprised.

She thrust her arms into her stained blue chambray work shirt as she headed for the kitchen and the coffee she hoped was almost finished brewing.

Her father had always been that way. Thinking she was just like her mother, when the reality of it was she was just like him! Wouldn't he be surprised when he found out he wasn't the only one in the family capable of striking oil!

Adrenaline pumping through her veins, Josie pulled the coffeepot off the warmer, rinsed out the stainless steel thermos and poured coffee in. She grabbed a couple of paper beverage cups, her flashlight and headed out the door. As her feet hit the ground and the door slammed behind her, the first big fat raindrop landed on her head. Josie thought about going back to find her windbreaker or her yellow rain slicker, then decided to heck with it. It was a warm summer night. She'd survive, even if she got a little wet. The important thing was to get over to the drilling rig and find out just why the round-the-clock drilling had stopped. This time.

Wade woke shortly after 5:00 a.m. with a gut feeling that something was wrong. Which, considering how things had been going so far on the trouble-laden drilling site, was not an unreasonable assumption. Having learned at a very early age to trust his instincts—especially when it came to business—he showered, dressed and, being careful not to wake his brother Shane, who was crashing in his guest room for the night, pulled on a Stetson and his yellow rain slicker and headed over to the site, where his worst suspicions were confirmed.

The drill was silent and motionless, and Josie and the rest of the team were hunkered down over the hole, peering down into the pipe. "Problem?" he asked as he strode through the driving rain and climbed up on the platform to join them.

Unlike Wade, none of them had on any rain gear and were, as a consequence, all soaked to the skin.

The three men and Josie looked at each other. Finally Josie stood and squared off with him. "The drill's stuck."

"How long?" Wade bit out, as Josie reached for a thermos and poured him what was left of the coffee, which amounted to about half a cup.

Josie looked at the men. Silent communication passed among them, and the collective misery on their faces told Wade, more than words ever could, how bad it was. Just as he knew, from one taste of the bitter, lukewarm liquid, who had made the coffee.

Josie squared her shoulders and stuck her hands in the back pockets of her jeans. Once again she took it upon herself to deliver the bad news. "Hours now. We've tried everything to get it out but so far nothing's working."

With stony resolve, Josie filled Wade in on everything that had been tried so far and everything that might possibly be tried next. Once again he was struck not just by her dogged determination to keep going despite the constant setbacks and aggravation, or the depth and breadth of her knowledge about drilling machinery and techniques, but the respect the men obviously had for her. Given her knowledge base, it was due to her, of course, but what he was feeling was a lot more than that, too, Wade knew. And as he had decided the evening before when talking to his younger brother Shane, maybe it was time they started dealing with that, too, Wade told himself grimly.

His expression deliberately closed and uncom-municative, Wade looked at Gus and the men. "Why don't you knock off until the rain lets up and get some breakfast." He frowned as the pager on his belt began to vibrate. He unclipped it and looked at the message floating across the screen. Saw a phone number and name, both of which he'd like to forget, followed by the cryptic and not unexpected message: Check your fax machine, you s.o.b.

"I've got to go back to my ranch house, catch some news, pick up a fax and make a few calls." Wade looked at Josie. "Then I'll be by to, uh, reassess." And clear a few things up.

Josie's tongue snaked out to wet her lower lip while the water continued to sluice down steadily on her head. For the first time since he'd arrived at the site, she looked nervous. Unaccountably so.

"Mind if I go with you?" she said, already heading for his truck, her long legs flashing in the rain. She tossed him a look over her shoulder as if it had been decided. "We can talk on the way."

Ignoring the stunned looks of Gus, Dieter and Ernie, Josie sloshed through the mud, yanked open the door and climbed in the passenger side of Wade's Expedi-tion getting rain and mud all over the rubber mat in the process.

To her relief, Wade followed, albeit a lot more insou-ciantly.

"You're soaked," he remarked, climbing in beside her. He also got mud and rain all over the rubber mat.

Not wanting him to see how desperate she was to divert him, Josie stared straight ahead. The way she figured it, the new South American oil field would be on the news for maybe twenty-four hours at the very most. So all she had to do was make sure that Wade didn't catch any of the world news—at least until the oil on his own land had come in.

Keeping him away from the newspapers and the cable television networks wouldn't be much of a problem. They didn't get cable that far out in the country. He didn't have a satellite dish. Nor did he have a newspaper delivered to him there, since he'd bought the Golden Slipper Ranch simply to acquire the mineral rights. Local radio programs carried ranch and farm reports, country music, the occasional religious program.

News via the Internet was something else again, however, since it was available on computer twenty-four hours a day. Plus, it was geared to national and international news, not local. So she'd have to keep him away from that, too.

Aware he was waiting for a response to his comment, she said casually, "It's not the first time I've been rained on." She turned to give him her most charming debutante smile. "I'll dry."

Noting the windows were steaming up from the combination of humidity, body heat and rain, Wade turned up the truck's air-conditioning a notch. He slowed down slightly and wiped the window in front of him with his sleeve. Then tore his eyes away from the gravel ranch road just long enough to study her with a sidelong glance.

Josie sort of smiled at him and nodded vaguely and tried not to get too agitated, even as she wondered guiltily if her withholding this information about the oil strike could be considered a lie, too.

The most famous Texas wildcatters had always been incredibly inventive and imaginative in compiling the resources they needed to succeed. But Josie didn't think any of her idols had been reduced to the shenanigans she was pulling. And while part of her thought she was foolish to be going so far out on a limb, she also knew everyone would forgive her in the end, when she did strike oil on the Golden Slipper Ranch. And then, with this success behind her, she would never be reduced to such tomfoolery again.

"So what did you want to talk to me about?" Wade said as he drove the short distance to the tiny white house with the gingerbread porch and turquoise shutters.

Best they didn't talk about the drilling until Gus, Ernie and Dieter had the drill unstuck and running again. Which left only one thing.

"That party you were planning for your folks," Josie said, her teeth beginning to chatter as the cool air coming from the vents permeated her soaked clothing.

Wade's glance narrowed as he reached over to turn it down a notch. "What about it?" he demanded lazily. Looking once again like he would never in a million years be able to figure her out.

Josie shrugged. "I was wondering if you needed any help, considering your events planner just quit and all."

"I'm about to find out." Wade pulled up next to a hopelessly beat-up red Ford pickup truck, parked as close to the front porch as he could and cut the motor on his Expedition.

He got out. So did Josie. Both sprinted through the driving rain to the front door. Their boots clattered up the front steps as a blond hunk, in denim jacket, shirt and jeans, boots and a remarkable familial resemblance to Wade McCabe came swaggering out.

"Company, and so early," he drawled, taking in Josie's wet, clinging clothes with a lascivious wink. "Brother, you impress me."

"My brother Shane," Wade murmured beneath his breath, making no effort to finish the introductions and give Shane Josie's name.

Shane looked at Wade, his demeanor serious. "I got property to look at. Some near. Some not so near. I won't be back for a couple of days, but I will be back in time for the surprise party on Friday."

Wade nodded as Shane used the flat of his hand to settle his hat more squarely across his brow. "Whatever you do, make sure the folks don't set me up with someone while I'm gone," Shane said.

Wade grinned mischievously, giving Josie her first clue as to what kind of brother he had been and still was. "Can't blame them for thinkin' you need help in that particular arena," he drawled.

Shane tilted his head Josie's way, keeping his own mischievously sparkling eyes on Wade all the while. "You just watch out for your own interests, pardner. I'll watch out for mine." Shane tipped his hat at Josie gallantly. "Keep him in line," he drawled. Then he stepped off the porch into the rain and dashed for his battered red pickup truck.

Wade shook the rain off his hat and massive shoulders, then led the way inside.

The air-conditioning hit Josie like a chilly Texas wind, sending yet another wave of icy shivers over her skin.

Wade switched on a light against the pale dawn, then turned and took one look at her, his glance sweeping down her body, lingering hotly, rapaciously over her breasts. "We have got," Wade growled determinedly, "to get you into some dry clothes."

Josie looked down and saw immediately what he meant. Soft, wet cotton was molded to her breasts, which were as clearly outlined as if she had been a contestant in a wet T-shirt contest.

Flushing, and feeling her nipples tighten all the more against the clinging cotton, she turned away.

His mouth set in a hard line, Wade disappeared up the stairs. She heard his boots moving across the floor. Drawers opening and shutting. A closet, too. Then he came back with a folded navy-blue sheet, blue chambray work shirt and a pair of thick cotton socks.

Averting his eyes, he thrust the booty into her arms and told her gruffly, "A hot shower would be the fastest way to warm up. Bathroom's at the top of the stairs. There are plenty of towels in there. If you put your clothes outside, I'll drop them in the dryer for you."

Josie couldn't deny she was chilled to the skin. A hot shower sounded wonderful. Holding the dry clothes in one hand, her soaked shirt away from her breasts with the other, she glanced surreptitiously down at her watch and noted it was six forty-five.

No national news was on the local television stations till seven. Which meant she had fifteen minutes to pull herself together, after which she needed to make sure he was so busy he had no time to find other sources of national news—like the Internet.

"I don't suppose I could trouble you for a cup of coffee, too. Maybe a little something to eat?"

Again Wade looked surprised. And with good reason, Josie thought. She was being awfully demanding of him. Fortunately he had obviously been too well brought up to deny a guest food and drink.

"No problem," he said easily, after only a slight hesitation. "I'll put some coffee on. Scrambled eggs and orange juice all right with you?"

Josie nodded and tried not to feel too embarrassed that she had just invited herself for breakfast at a client's home. "Perfect."

She hurried up the stairs, her clothes smacking wetly against her as she moved.

The hot shower helped take away the chills. Unfortunately she couldn't linger in it. Drying off quickly, she slipped on the thick white socks, then straightening, grabbed the navy-blue sheet and tucked it beneath her armpits, wrapping it around her repeatedly so it covered her from chest to toes. She secured it firmly by tucking the end between her breasts, then slipped on the long blue chambray shirt, which fell almost to her knees, and knotted the ends together at her waist. Running a comb through her hair, she blow-dried it briefly and secured it away from her face. With five minutes left to spare, she hurried back downstairs.

Wade was at the stove, pushing eggs around in a skillet. "Pour us both a cup of coffee, will you?" he said without turning around.

Josie was relieved to note the television in the small kitchen was silent.

Feeling guilty about the way she was imposing on him, she rushed to do his bidding. "Sure. You take cream or sugar in yours?"

"Milk. And it's in the fridge. Sugar is in the bowl in the cupboard just above the coffee."

"Gotcha."

The toast popped up. He tossed one piece on each plate, put two more pieces in. By the time he'd poured juice for both of them and transferred the eggs to the plates, the second two pieces of toast were ready. He added them to the plates, carried them to the table and sat down opposite her.

"Wow," was all Josie could say. "You do know how to cook."

Wade shrugged. "Eggs, steak and coffee. That's about the extent of it. You?"

"Let's just say you've probably got me beat." Josie lifted the coffee to her lips and drank deeply of the steaming hot, fragrant liquid. It was without a doubt the best she'd ever had. And it put hers to shame. "The coffee is incredible. What do you do to make it taste so good?"

He grinned at her unrepentantly. "Follow directions on the can?"

"Very funny. And I'm serious." Josie shifted positions. Their knees collided beneath the table. Swiftly she drew her legs back. But that did nothing to stop the tingling that was ghosting upward from her knees, through her thighs, to her tummy. "I don't know why mine always tastes so bad."

He added jam to his toast and salt and pepper to his eggs with more than necessary care. "Did you make it this morning?"

Josie nodded.

Wade forked up eggs and munched on them. He looked like he had a lot more than cooking on his mind. "I'm guessing you didn't use the right ratio of coffee to water."

"Oh." Josie flushed, embarrassed.

"But you didn't come here to talk about how to make coffee," he reminded, his gaze raking the length of her before returning to her face. "You want to talk about the drilling problems. And as it happens," he told her heavily, "so do I."

Josie didn't like the sound of that. Not at all. Telling herself not to appear panicked, she dug into her breakfast, forced herself to swallow some of the delicious, fluffy eggs.

Wade drummed his fingers on the tabletop. "I've got to tell you, Josie. If it were anyone else but the Wyatt Drilling Company on this project, I'd pull the plug. Right now."

Josie's heart skipped a beat. The bite of scrambled eggs she'd just eaten lay like a hunk of wood in her stomach. She forced herself to meet his gaze. "But you're not going to do that, are you?" she whispered hoarsely.

Wade shrugged and continued to regard her steadily. "That all depends."

Josie swallowed hard around the growing knot of emotion in her throat. "On what?"

"On whether or not you plan to start being honest with me."

Chapter 7

"I don't know what you mean," Josie stammered.

"Yes, Josie," Wade said, still eyeing her with a depth of male speculation Josie found very disturbing, "you do."

Josie jumped up from the table and moved about the kitchen restlessly. "I've been frank with you about the problems we've been having on the site."

Wade pushed away from the table, too. He stood with his feet braced slightly apart. He jammed his hands on his hips and narrowed his eyes.

"But you haven't been frank with me about your role in the project," he told her smoothly. "It's obvious to me—and would be to anyone else with half a brain—that you're a lot more than an entry-level gofer or record keeper on this project. You're integrally involved with—if not actually in charge of—all the decisions that are going on, with possibly even more say than Gus." He paused, looking her up and down from the top of her mussed hair to her toes. "What I don't understand is why you're pretending you're not."

One very good reason, Josie thought uncomfortably, her dad knew nothing about this entire project. And would, in fact, probably kick her butt from here to Abilene if he were to find out before they actually hit oil. After…well, after she could only hope that her dad and everyone else would understand why she'd done what she had. Otherwise, she was going to be in very big trouble indeed.

Doing her best to keep a level head, Josie shrugged. She folded her arms in front of her matter-of-factly. She could feel the blood rushing to her cheeks, even as she struggled to get a handle on her soaring emotions.

"This is still a business dominated by men. There are a few women actively involved in the wildcatting business, but for the most part it's still a boy's club, especially here in Texas."

"And you want to join," Wade guessed, searching her eyes with his.

Josie nodded, relieved to be able to candidly confess, "Enough to have swallowed my pride and taken a ridiculously low entry-level position with Big Jim just to get a toehold in the business." It still galled her that that had been necessary.

Wade studied her. "Does Big Jim know the extent of your ambitions?"

"Yes." Josie retrieved the coffeepot and topped off both their cups with more of Wade's hot, delicious coffee. "He just doesn't think much of my expertise—

yet. But I'm going to prove him wrong on that with my input in this job," Josie told him determinedly.

Wade folded his arms in front of him and rested both his elbows on the table. "So your position here really is…?" he asked, keeping his eyes on hers.

Josie felt herself flushing under his continued scrutiny.

"Officially, as far as Big Jim goes, my position is just as lowly as I've said. Unofficially, well, let's just say that Gus, Dieter and Ernie have all come to realize how much I really do know about the business and I, in turn, have welcomed the opportunity to share everything I learned at my dad's elbow with them on this job. Hopefully, when we strike oil, and Big Jim understands the pivotal role I've played in our success, he'll share that happiness, too, and give me a lot more responsibility." At least she hoped so, Josie thought, as she cradled her coffee cup to her chest.

"Which brings us to the next point," Wade said, casting a glance out the window. Noticing it had stopped raining, he picked up his coffee cup and escorted her onto the back porch. Cottony blue-gray clouds were streaking across the Texas sky, being buffeted about by a cool wind. The sun, surrounded by a starburst of pink, rose slowly in the east. "I'm thinking—considering this latest fiasco—that maybe it's time we reassessed. And wait for Big Jim to get back from his consulting job in South America before we continue."

Josie sighed her frustration. She took a long, slow sip of coffee. Although she had braced herself for just this eventuality, she had hoped it wouldn't happen. Not that it really mattered. She had promised the guys that she'd give them time to get the drill up and running again. She was going to keep that promise.

Josie drained the rest of her coffee in a single draught. She looked him straight in the eye. "Not," she said firmly, leading the way back inside and setting her cup aside, "before I show you something first."

Josie's clothes were dry. While she plucked them from the dryer and hurried off to dress, Wade went to check the fax machine for the fax that had supposedly come in earlier. As she came down the stairs, he was still on the phone. To his chagrin, the news was not good. "I understand," he said in a low, grim tone. "Thanks. Some other time." Without another word he hung up the phone and swung around to face her.

It was a relief to have her out of the sheet-and-shirt ensemble, to know she was no longer nearly naked beneath. It was all he'd been able to do earlier to keep his imagination in check—to stop from mentally disrobing her and making love to her, again and again and again.

Not that seeing her in jeans, T-shirt and work shirt was any less seductive, particularly when he knew—both from the way her breasts jiggled softly as she moved and the clothes he'd put in the dryer—that her panties consisted of a surprisingly delicate triangle of satin and lace, and she'd forgone wearing a bra.

Not that he had any business thinking of her this way, he reminded himself firmly. Or wondering how she would react if he gave in to his baser impulses, took her in his arms, undressed her slowly and kissed her senseless.

Josie focused on his expression. "Problem?" she

asked curiously. Boots in hand, she sat down on the next-to-bottom step.

Wade frowned. He swallowed around the unaccustomed dryness of his throat, pushed the image of Josie—naked in his bed—from his mind. He was not going to find out how her hair would look spread across his pillow or know how soft and beautiful she was all over.

Aware she was still waiting for an answer and that she thought his peculiar mood related to the phone call, he replied, "Remember Andrea?"

Josie nodded. "The events planner who left you high and dry."

Wade nodded, his attention shifting to the problem at hand. "Not only has she been tracking my progress at making arrangements for the party myself, but she has apparently prevailed upon all her colleagues in Houston to make sure I don't get help from any of the best caterers or florists. Apparently Andrea and her friends have decided to make an example out of me."

Josie made a sympathetic face as she worked her foot into the top of her red Western boot. "Have you considered using local merchants?"

Wade watched in fascination as Josie gripped the sides of her boot with both hands and simultaneously extended her long luscious showgirl leg away from her body. Her foot made a soft, swishing sound as it connected snugly with the sole. "Like you said," Wade drawled, wishing her jeans weren't quite so tight, her bottom so enticingly rounded, "it's June. There are four weddings earlier in the day in Laramie, six at various churches on Friday evening and even more on Sunday.

Needless to say, the area merchants already have their hands full. I know, 'cause I tried them first."

Josie paused. Leaning forward, she rested the inside of her forearm on her knee and regarded him with bright-eyed speculation. "Have you tried Fort Worth or Dallas merchants?"

"That's next on my list." Struggling to keep his mind on the conversation, Wade wiped a bead of perspiration from his upper lip. "But where—and with whom—to start is a mystery to me. I've never thrown any parties in that part of the state." The few he'd had, had always been in Houston.

Josie smiled at him confidently. "I know a few people there who arrange parties," she told him reassuringly. "A couple of 'em even owe me a favor or two or three." Josie extended her other leg and shoved her foot all the way into her boot in the same, deliberate, incredibly sensual, easy-to-watch process. Finished, she bounded cheerfully to her feet, slapped her hands on her hips and looked him straight in the eye. "I'll be happy to help hook you up with them. But first—" she linked arms with him, the softness of her breasts lightly brushing his arm "—we've got to go out and do what we should have done first and look at the property."

Figuring he owed her that much, Wade let Josie chart their expedition. She stopped by her trailer to get a topology map of the surrounding area and the property Wade owned. With Josie charting the way, they drove, then walked along the creek that wound through the Golden Slipper Ranch, studying the bends and the curves of the snaking waterbed now filled nearly to overflowing with the results of the previous night's rain.

Together they noted the surface formations that—according to the "creekology" method pioneered by legendary wildcatter Hugh Roy Cullen and used extensively by Big Jim—indicated oil formations below. From there they visited several other sites in the general area where wells had been dug years before only to go dry shortly thereafter without producing much. Finally they went back to the desolate area where Josie and her team had decided to drill.

Standing a good distance back from the steel rig, where Ernie, Gus and Dieter were now working again, Josie turned and looked at Wade and said, "What do you see?"

Wade sighed and shrugged, his glance on the men on the drilling rig, who still had yet to get the drill going again. "A lost cause?" he guessed dryly.

Josie scowled. "Besides the current problem," she said impatiently. Hands on her slender hips, she turned to face him.

Wade looked at the desolate landscape peppered with trees. Heaven knew, as grazing land it had never been worth much. Truth to tell, this particular section of his ranch wasn't much to look at, either. "Cacti, scrub brush, cedar, mesquite—"

"I'm not talking vegetation," Josie replied, looking irked. "I'm talking terrain."

Reluctantly Wade turned his attention from her, to the topography.

"A flat area surrounding a big hill."

Josie smiled, like a teacher regarding a particularly

brilliant student. "Now, stand over here and take a deep breath and tell me what you smell," she directed enthusiastically.

Wade drew a deep breath. "Sulphur."

"Very good." Her lusciously soft, bare lips forming a beautiful smile, Josie picked up some soggy dirt in her fist and transferred it to his palm. "And what is this?" she asked cheerfully.

Wade glanced down at the juxtaposition of her soft, delicate hands over his larger, rougher ones. "A mixture of mud, clay and sand."

Josie's grin widened. "In the history of Texas oil finds, what other big well had all these properties?" she quizzed enthusiastically, wiping her hands down the sides of her jeans.

"Spindletop." Wade dropped the muddy soil back onto the ground and watched as Josie sensually scrubbed as much dirt as she could from her palms on her jeans.

"Bingo!" Josie said. She watched him rub the dirt from his hand the same way. "Not to mention the creekology fits," she said eagerly, striding closer. "And the property also has significant underground deposits of sandstone and shale."

"I know all that," Wade said dryly as the increasingly warm breeze stirred shimmery dark brown strands of Josie's hair. "I acquired this land and the oil and gas leases for it for that very reason," he told her as he drank in the scent of her. "Because it looked promising."

Josie planted her dirt-stained hands on her hips and

tilted her chin up. "Then why are you so willing to give up now?" she demanded.

"Not give up," Wade corrected, aware he would've liked nothing more at that moment than to haul her into his arms and kiss her again and again. "Put it on hold till Big Jim gets back," he finished explaining his point of view firmly.

Josie's chin thrust out mutinously. "We can do this, Wade," she said.

"I know you think you can, Josie," he said gently.

"But you're not convinced." Hurt resonated in Josie's eyes.

"No." He paused, knowing he should keep his emotions—his attraction to Josie—out of this equation. He knew full well business and pleasure did not mix. But he was unable to turn off his attraction to Josie, any more than he was able to curtail his growing desire to hold her in his arms and kiss her passionately again. "But you are," he observed softly, wanting more than ever to understand her. "Why?"

"I'm not sure I can explain." Josie turned away, looking uneasy again. Like she was afraid to reveal too much about herself to him.

Wade put his hands on her shoulders and turned her back to face him. He wanted them to trust each other, and the only way that would happen was if they also understood each other. In their business and their personal lives. "Try."

Josie nudged the base of a cactus with her foot. Her expression became reflective. "My dad used to talk about what made the early independents successful. He said knowing where to dig was a combination of science, financial considerations and intuition." The edge of her white teeth raked across the plumpness of her soft, bare lower lip. "I've seen Big Jim work—he has this amazing ability to figure out where the oil is. I'll be honest with you," Josie said softly, lifting her eyes to his with the trusting confession he'd been seeking. "I think I've got it, too."

Josie waited for Wade to scoff, laugh or otherwise belittle or make fun of her like so many others had. To her relief he did none of those things.

"And you feel it here," he noted, continuing to study her resolutely. Compassion lit his eyes.

Josie nodded. "So strongly I can't even begin to describe it," she whispered. She paused, worrying her lower lip with her teeth, and looked deep into his eyes, finding all the understanding-and respect—she ever could have wanted there. "You don't seem surprised," she noted softly. In fact, unlike so many others, he didn't doubt her at all.

Wade shrugged. "Maybe because I've got the same ability—in financial matters." He took one of her hands in his and led her over to the back of his truck. He opened up the back. Hands on her waist, he lifted her up to sit with her legs hanging off the tailgate of the truck, then hoisted himself up to sit beside her. "I learned very early that I had a real knack for sizing up likely financial outcomes of any given situation."

Josie relaxed beside him. "How young?"

Wade smiled, recollecting. He grabbed the thermos of orange juice they'd brought with them and poured some into the stainless steel cap that also doubled as a drinking cup. "I was eight when I began collecting stamps and coins." His hand brushed hers as he handed her the icy cold juice. He watched as she lifted it to her lips and drank deeply.

"I started trading those, made a profit, and when I was ten used those proceeds to buy my first stock," Wade continued filling her in companionably. "My folks used to shake their heads—they didn't know where I got my intense interest in all things financial— but they were really great about it, too, in encouraging my interests. They let me get a paper route and invest all my earnings in whatever I chose."

"Which was…?" Josie drained the cup.

"Gold, silver, more stocks and savings bonds." Wade lifted the cup to his lips and took a sip. "I wanted a diverse portfolio even then."

"Amazing," Josie murmured.

"Nope." Wade grinned. "Just me." Wade knew he had plenty of shortcomings to balance his talents. Plenty of them. But he was still proud of what he had accomplished and, for reasons he wasn't sure he wanted to examine closely, eager to share his experiences with Josie. "By the time I was in college I had so many things going I could pay my own way," he admitted, aware it was going to be a blistering-hot day after all, despite the cooling rain they'd had just hours before.

"That must have delighted your parents." Josie swung her legs back and forth, like a kid pumping a swing.

Wade looked at the way Josie had braced her hands on either side of her, her fingers curling around the edge of the truck bed. "With four sons to support and put through college, you bet it did. Anyway," he tilted his head to the side, "afterward I was too busy overseeing my various investments to hold a regular job. And financially—because I'd been so careful to pick only top-returning investments—there was no need for me to do that. I had more than enough to live on and reinvest, and that's when I branched out and began acquiring oil and gas leases, too."

Josie sighed admiringly. "You're really something."

"So are you." Wade gave in to the impulse and covered her hand with his own. He paused, delighting in the soft, warm feel of her skin and the pulse throbbing in her wrist. "I don't think I've ever met a woman quite like you."

Josie mugged at him and made no effort to pull away. "I'll take that as a compliment."

Were they flirting here? How had that happened? Wade wondered.

He had never been one to let business discussions veer off into the personal.

"Now—" Josie drew a deep, energizing breath and smiled "—to continue our discussion." Her eyes glimmered merrily as she turned slightly to face him. She pointed a finger at him, like a professor addressing the class. "You know that with any given discovery well there are at least four dozen things that can go wrong during the drilling process."

Wade rolled his eyes, loving the excited color that had come into her high, sculpted cheeks. "At least."

Josie leaned toward him intimately. "And, to pick up your lesson in the history of Texas wildcatting—you do know who Hugh Roy Cullen was, don't you?"

Wade nodded. "Absolutely."

"Then you probably also know his motto?" Josie guessed.

"Dig a Little Deeper than Anyone Else."

Josie grinned, looking sexy as hell. "That, cowboy, is exactly what I think we should do."

In the distance there was a whoop at the derrick, then a thumbs-up from Gus and the guys as the drill got going again. Josie grinned, gave a thumbs-up back, and slapped Wade on the thigh. "Is that a sign or what?" she crowed gleefully.

Sign or no, Wade soon found himself agreeing to let Josie and the team continue drilling the discovery well in Big Jim's absence. That settled, and with everything well under control at the site, Josie insisted they get down to work on the party for his parents.

"I just need to change into some clean clothes," Josie told Wade as she led the way into her trailer. "The only problem is," Josie said, as she sidestepped the huge pile of laundry on the floor and sifted through the empty drawers in her bedroom and the row of empty hangers in her closet, "I don't have anything clean left."

Wade lounged in the doorway to her bedroom. Josie wasn't sure how and when they had got so comfortable with each other, she just knew that they had, and that she liked it—maybe a lot more than she should.

He studied the disarray with cheerful disdain. "Looks like you could use some help. Come on. Gather up your clothes and we'll take them over to the ranch house and you can do laundry there while we work on the party arrangements."

Josie sighed. "I've got to admit I wouldn't mind taking care of two things at once." Particularly since she had no idea when she'd have time to take everything to the coin laundry in Laramie.

"Good. Then it's settled." He winked. "Hell, if you can find me a caterer for Friday night, I may even teach you how to make a great cup of coffee."

Josie shoved her laundry into three big duffel-style laundry bags. "You just keep dreaming, cowboy."

"I just may."

While Wade tossed her laundry into the back of his Expedition, Josie went over to have a word with Gus. He used a red bandana to wipe the perspiration from his face while she filled him in on her plans.

"McCabe doesn't know about the oil strike in South America yet, does he?" Gus growled as protectively as any father, as soon as she had finished.

"No," Josie retorted stubbornly, feeling a lecture she most certainly did not want to hear coming on. "And with any luck at all, he won't until after we strike oil here, too."

"You're taking a big risk, keeping him in the dark this way," Gus predicted direly.

Especially, Josie thought, when she was also getting close to him.

But she couldn't think about that now.

"One thing at a time," Josie told Gus firmly as she headed away from the drilling rig. "And right now I've got to help Wade plan a party."

"I can't believe we managed to take care of everything in under three hours," Wade said. "Caterer, florist, orchestra, videographer, photographer, even parking valets. It's all arranged."

It wasn't hard, Josie thought, when you knew exactly what you wanted and exactly who to call. She got up from the kitchen table and went into the adjacent laundry room to retrieve the second load of clothes from the dryer. "You're right." She transferred the warm, fragrant clothes from the dryer to the long rectangular worktable adjacent to it. Then added the clothes in the washer to the dryer, threw in a fabric softener sheet and switched it on. "We really lucked out."

"It was more than luck," Wade said admiringly as Josie moved lithely back to the worktable. "I watched you talk to those people. You've done this before."

Josie knew she had inherited her mother's talent for throwing one humdinger of a party as surely as she had inherited her dad's talent for sniffing out oil, but it wasn't where her heart was.

Deciding to go with her gut and tell him as much as she could about herself without revealing something that would get her fired, she smiled at him and said vaguely, "I made arrangements for a lot of parties and fund-raisers as part of my previous job."

"Which was...?" Wade plucked a towel from the stack and folded that while Josie smoothed the wrinkles from a steady stream of warm T-shirts.

"Coordinator of special projects at a charitable foundation in Dallas."

"But you weren't happy doing that," Wade observed, picking up another towel.

"No." Josie untangled a lacy bra from a matching satin panty. "And I realized after putting almost seven years into my job there that I was never going to be. Don't get me wrong." She plucked a silk teddy from the mound of freshly laundered clothes. "I like being part of something that did so much good in terms of helping so many people in so many different ways. The foundation sponsored many wonderful things—school programs for indigent children, grants for starving artists, college scholarships, medical research. And they spent a lot of time bringing public attention to issues and raising additional money for the various projects, too."

"Sounds like a challenging job."

Josie nodded, aware on one level it had been very fulfilling. "It was," she admitted softly.

"But?"

Josie grimaced as she mated the socks. "My mother worked at the same place."

Wade raised a brow. Noting a lacy bra had slipped to the floor, he reached over and retrieved it. "Is that why you got the job?"

Josie tried not to blush as Wade folded the bra and added it to her growing stack of lingerie. "I'd like to say it was totally because of my own talent for dealing with people and making things happen, but my mother chairs the foundation, so she has a lot of say in what goes on there, so that was part of it, too."

"Was it hard, working in the same place as your mother?" he asked.

Not nearly as hard as selectively editing what I tell you, Josie thought, pining for the day when she could simply tell him everything.

"As you saw by the pretty dress she sent me, she can

be a tad overwhelming in trying to get me to do what she wants," Josie said dryly.

Wade grinned in a way that reminded Josie he had some overbearing mother problems of his own. "Which is...?"

Josie made a rueful face. "Marry someone rich and pedigreed and settle down and have a family."

Wade studied her, no expression readily apparent on his face. "But you don't want that?"

Josie shook her head. "Not the rich, pedigreed part, no."

"But you do want a husband and family," Wade observed quietly, his brown eyes softening understandingly.

"Yes," Josie admitted, surprised to discover how much she had begun to want just that in the last couple of days. "Someday—when I've proven myself in the oil fields—I do." She paused, knowing she shouldn't ask, but unable to help herself. "What about you?" she prodded softly. "Do you ever plan to marry?"

Chapter 8

"You don't have a problem asking questions, do you?" Wade said. He was so close she could feel the heat and tension emanating from his tall body.

Josie began piling the stacks of clothes into the bottom of the duffel-style laundry bag she had brought with her. "Do you have a problem answering them?"

Wade rested a hip on the edge of the worktable. "I'm not necessarily interested in marriage per se. I'd like to have a personal life as satisfying as my professional life, but it could be a lifelong love affair."

Josie had never imagined herself satisfied with that. Maybe it was because she had come from a broken home, but when she committed herself to a man, she would want him to make the commitment of marriage and then stick with it, through thick and thin.

"What about kids?" she asked softly, trying not to

feel too disappointed that Wade was not as old-fashioned as she was in that regard. "Do you want them?"

He watched as she shifted the duffel bag to a far corner of the table. Half his mouth lifted in a rakish smile. "Do you?"

Josie could tell by the way he was looking at her that a lot was riding on her answer. And indeed everything she said and did. "Someday," she replied honestly. Still holding his eyes, she amended with a shrug, "I don't know how easy it will be to work out, given the career I want, but yes," she admitted slowly, thoughtfully, "I do."

Wade studied her. Pleasure lit his eyes. "I imagine if anyone can work it out, you can," he told her in a low, husky voice.

"Thanks," Josie murmured, wishing she didn't recall quite so vividly just how well he kissed or how gallantly he held her in his arms. She wished she didn't want him to kiss her again, but she did. And judging by the way he was looking at her, he wanted to kiss her, too.

Josie cleared her throat and edged away from him. "And you didn't answer my question," she said mildly, as she led the way back into the kitchen. "Do you want kids?"

Wade followed her, his steps long and lazy. "Up until now, I haven't, no," he replied candidly. But that was beginning to change now that Josie was in his life. And no one was more surprised about that than he.

Disappointment glimmered briefly in her eyes. Wordlessly she turned on her heel and returned to the kitchen to rinse out her coffee cup.

Determined to lighten the mood and return to their

previous camaraderie, he followed her to the sink, plucked the coffee cup from her hand, and put it in the dishwasher. He shut the dishwasher, then turned to face her. "Of course if you're going to be a mom," he drawled playfully, "you're going to have to improve your skills in the kitchen or your babies are going to starve."

Josie leaned a slender hip against the sink. She folded her arms in front of her. "Back to reforming me again?" she taunted mutinously.

Wade noted that even though her arms were crossed tightly in a defensive position in front of her, she wasn't trying to get away from him anymore. He took solace in that. "I'd like to think the process is ongoing and mutual," he murmured, stroking his hands from her shoulders to her elbows.

Josie studied him but didn't pull away. "And how am I reforming you?" Josie challenged softly.

By helping him open up. He'd barely known her three days and had already told her more about himself and his feelings than he'd told anyone else in his adult life. That alone was nothing short of a miracle. And there was a part of him—the part that was starved for true intimacy with another human being—that very much wanted to find out just how much closer, how much more open with each other the two of them could get.

But figuring that was a little much to lay on her so soon after they'd met, figuring it might even sound a little fake, as if he were trying to feed her a line to get her into bed with him, Wade merely shrugged and said, "Teaching me how to go more by my gut." In matters of the heart, he thought, and— "When it comes to finding oil."

Again something flashed in her eyes. Hurt—disappointment that he wasn't more forthcoming—then was gone. "I probably should get going," she said. She brushed past him, her head tipped up regally. "Maybe I could come back later and get the clothes from the dryer?"

"Sure." It was all Wade could do not to catch her by the waist and bring her back to his side. Then again, maybe they'd gotten close enough for one afternoon, anyway, he thought. He glanced at his watch, murmured thoughtfully, "I need to check today's stocks and bonds, anyway." He couldn't believe it was as late as it was and he hadn't checked once. Usually by noon he had already tracked his investments and possibly done some trades, several times.

Josie stopped dead in her tracks. She pivoted slowly to face him with a tomboy's feisty grace and her own inherent style. Though she'd been going for hours now, she still looked as lovely as she had that morning. Her dark hair was caught in a high bouncy ponytail on her head. Her face bore the golden glow of the sun and her cheeks were flushed pink. She'd never had time—or opportunity—to put on a bra, and her breasts moved softly beneath her T-shirt whenever she did. She didn't seem aware of it, though, any more than she was aware how enticingly her jeans cloaked her slender hips, waist, thighs and calves. But he was aware of it. So aware he'd been aching with the desire to make her his all day.

"How do you do that?" Josie asked, almost too casually. "Do you call your broker?"

Wade tried not to let on how restless and edgy he felt. "No. I do it myself—on the Internet. Here," he continued matter-of-factly. "I'll show you."

"You don't have to do that," Josie said hastily, suddenly beginning to look a little panicked. "In fact, if you could just take me back to the site—"

Wade didn't want her to go. In fact, for reasons he didn't want to look too closely at he was damn near desperate for her to stay.

He took her gallantly by the wrist and led her over to the desk where his laptop modem was plugged into the phone line. "It's no problem," he told her easily. Wade guided her onto the seat of the chair. Standing over her, he reached around from behind her and switched the computer on. Seconds later the icons representing the various computer programs popped up on the screen. Wade guided the computer cursor to the icon that characterized Internet services and clicked on it. Seconds later, the front page of that day's edition of *USA Daily* newspaper popped up on screen. But Wade barely saw it, so immersed was he in the alluring fragrance of Josie's hair and skin.

Josie's heart took a giant leap as she scanned down rapidly and saw the sixth headline of the day. Major South American Oil Strike. Knowing fast action was called for, she accidentally-on-purpose hit the power button on the side of Wade's laptop. Without warning, the screen flashed a brilliant emerald green, then went black.

"What the—?" He started to reach for the power switch again.

Josie moved between Wade and his arm. Surging gracefully to her feet, she stood between Wade and the computer screen. "You know what?" she said in a light, flirtatious tone she had used a lot in her debutante days. She flattened her hands on his chest and toyed with the button on his shirt. "I don't think I need to see that."

Wade grinned and reached around her, letting her know with a sexy once-over she had successfully commanded his full attention. "But I wanted to show it to you," he said.

And chance the same headlines coming up all over again? Josie thought. No way.

"What I want you to show me," Josie said, moving forward, into his arms, as she continued to impede his reach, "is this."

Desperate times, Josie thought as she pushed Wade back against the wall, called for desperate measures. And heaven knew, she thought as she went up on tiptoe and laced her hands around his head, she was desperate to keep Wade from reading the day's headlines. So she put everything she had into the impromptu kiss, fitting her lips to his, slanting her head at just the right angle, and gently—experimentally—caressing his tongue and teeth. She expected gentleness, acquiescence. She got none. His lips were hard and hungry, his tongue hot and wet and unbearably sweet. He swept the insides of her mouth, languidly at first, then with growing passion, until she was lost in the touch, taste and feel of him, lost in the ragged intake of his breath and her own low, shuddering moan.

As the kiss deepened, Josie tried to convince herself she was merely coming on to Wade to buy time and achieve success. Merely trying to quench her desire and satisfy her curiosity about the sexiest, most compelling man she had ever met. But even as she rationalized her behavior and made excuses for her unprecedented wantonness, even as her hands curled in his rumpled hair, she knew it wasn't true.

She had fallen in love with Wade McCabe, even if she wasn't the woman of his dreams. And though her cautious side would dictate waiting to make love until she knew his feelings mirrored hers, the more reckless, lonely side of her could not walk away from the opportunity to be with him like this. She had wasted too much time in her life already, doing what everyone else wanted her to do.

She'd made the decision to follow her dreams, to start taking risks, and now that she had finally started taking them in her professional life, she was going to follow her heart and take them in her private life, too.

Wade hadn't expected Josie to kiss him. He hadn't expected any of this, he thought as he continued to claim her, and her soft, delicate hands caressed his shoulders and chest with slow, seductive strokes. But given what he knew about her, maybe he should have, Wade thought, as the sweet urgency of her tongue swept through him in hot, undulating waves. Josie was an inherently adventurous woman who until now, by her own admission, had been keeping herself—her ambition, her lust for life, her need for passion and the physical side of love—under tight wraps.

Now that she was finally allowing herself to take some risks, to meet him boldly kiss for kiss, she was as eager to please as she was reckless in her quest for success. Unfortunately she was also stubborn in her methods and—if his instincts were correct—woefully inexperienced when it came to men. And that, more than anything, gave the gentleman in Wade pause. He'd been brought up to never ever take advantage.

Conscience stinging, he lifted his head.

Josie gasped and clung. "Don't stop."

Wade groaned, reveling in the soft surrender of the lithe body pressed against the rock-hard demand of his.

"You say that now," he murmured, hauling her against him just long enough to make his point. But something happened when his mouth touched hers again. Maybe it was chemistry. Maybe it was love. He didn't know. He only knew he had never felt like this before. So connected—so quickly. So free of heart. He'd never wanted so very much to please. Never known he could delight so in a woman's soft body pressed against his.

The blood thundered through him, pooling low. Much more of this and there would be no turning back, not for either of them. Determined to do the right thing, Wade tightened his grip on her and tore his lips from hers. "Josie." He caught his breath and warned, "If you keep this up—"

Too far gone to care, Josie pressed her breasts against his chest and kissed him again—not just in surrender—but with an urgency and a need to please him that rocked him to his soul. "What, Wade? What will happen?" she whispered against his mouth.

"This," Wade said. He swept her against him and kissed her until he felt her tremble in response. Delighting in his victory, in the sweet vulnerability of her response, Wade pressed his sex into the cradle of her legs and covered her breasts with his hands. Her nipples peaked and she moaned against his mouth. Desire thundering through him in waves, he flattened the hard length of his body against the softness of hers. The contact wasn't enough, not nearly, Wade thought as he slowly, reluctantly, ended the kiss and gazed down at her. Her lips were wet and swollen from their kisses. Her eyes glowed with a soft, ardent gleam. "I'd give anything to be able to invite you up to my bed," he whispered huskily. He'd give anything to make her his woman—now—this afternoon. But it was too soon.

Josie sighed, her breath coming every bit as raggedly and erratically as his. "So why don't you?"

"Because," Wade said, struggling between his desire to protect her and his desire to make mad, passionate love to her, here and now and damn the consequences. "You're not the kind of woman who has flings."

"But I've dreamed of being this kind of woman, dreamed of being swept away," Josie protested softly.

Wade frowned. "Everyone does—to a point. It doesn't mean it should happen here and now." Because that left them open to the kind of regrets that could put a halt to everything. But Josie apparently did not see it that way, he noted.

"But not everyone is brave enough to follow their heart's desire." Josie's chin jutted out stubbornly. Wade didn't have to be a psychic to know what was on her mind. Worse, the same thing was on his, and had been all day.

Aware his lower half was still throbbing hotly, Wade

backed her to the wall. Hands braced on either side of her, he spread his legs on either side of hers, aligned his lower half with hers and slowly pressed his chest to hers. "For good reason."

"For no reason." Josie clutched at his shoulders like a woman who was in full command of her destiny. "And I meant what I said earlier, Wade." Color flooding her cheeks, she threaded her hands through his hair and swiftly, purposefully brought his head down to hers. "Don't stop," she murmured passionately as she stood on tiptoe and pressed her lips to his. She moved her hips against his insistently and delivered a deep, demanding kiss. "For once in my life, I want to be swept away. And I want you to do it."

Wade didn't want Josie to be left wanting, with any fantasy—any Cinderella dreams she might have—unfulfilled. He wanted her to have everything her heart desired. And because he did, he swept her up in his arms, carried her up to the master bedroom and sat her gently on the edge of his bed. He knelt before her, positioning himself between her thighs.

Unbuttoning and unzipping as he went, he kissed her long and hard and deep. Kissed her until she moaned softly in the back of her throat and his blood began to boil.

He slipped off her denim shirt. She took off her T-shirt. Wade sucked in his breath at the first sight of her lustrous golden skin. Her breasts were high and full—softly rounded globes with dusky rose centers, her waist slender. Wade hadn't known he could want anyone so desperately, but he did. He swiftly divested her of her boots and socks and jeans. Leaving her clad only in a pair of lacy panties, he kissed his way down her neck, sensually exploring the delicate U of her collarbone, her shoulders and arms, the insides of her elbows and wrists and finally the uppermost curves of her breasts. Not content with just seeing her, he cupped the weight of her breasts in his hands, brushed his thumbs across the tips. Once, and then again and again until she moaned.

Loving the way she trembled, the way she looked at him as if she had known—right from the minute they'd laid eyes on each other—they would end up this way, he bent his head and traced the rosy areola of her breast with his tongue, brushed it dry with his lips, then suckled her tenderly. Eager to please her, needing to know all of her, he moved to her other breast, working it to the same aroused state before continuing with his slow, sensual exploration and moving ever downward. Across her ribs, to her navel. Lower still, to the silky skin of her knees and the sleekness of her inner thighs. Her head fell back as he reached the dark, tri-angle of curls. He hooked his hands in the triangular scrap of lace. One hand curved around the nest of sable curls. The other flattened against the small of her spine. Cradled between the warmth of his hands, she arched against him. He stroked her repeatedly, light butterfly touches that had her shuddering. Moving up, in. Until she twisted against him, no longer able to bear it. Until she shook with her need for him and made a low, whim-pering plea. "Wade...Wade..."

Sliding his hands beneath her, he divested her of her panties, then guided her thighs apart. Driven by the same frantic need as she, he removed his clothes, then still kissing her passionately, draped his body over hers and lifted her against him. Taking everything she offered, and giving her everything in return, he surged into her slowly, deliberately. Gasping in pleasure, she wrapped her arms and legs around him, holding him close. While he continued with deep, then shallow strokes. Repeating the slow, deliberate exploration until she was breathing frantically and reaching for some distant, lofty point.

Suddenly she was there, catapulting over the edge, shuddering in release. And so was he.

Her body still humming with pleasure, Josie shut her eyes and buried her head in his chest. She literally could not believe she had done that. She could not believe they both had done that. And yet she could feel how much he needed and wanted her. How much she needed and wanted him. The heat of their joining had enveloped her in a pleasure unlike any she had ever known. Like a whirlwind, the fierceness of their love-making had swept them both into its power.

"I know what you're thinking, Josie," Wade murmured languidly at length as he stroked a hand down her spine and guided her closer still.

Josie nestled closer. "What?"

"That this all happened damn fast," Wade soothed, accurately reading her mind. "And yet—" hands on her shoulders, he brought her around to face him "—in retrospect, I wouldn't have it any other way." He shook his head in a mixture of awe and tender commemoration. "You and me, together like that. That was magic, Josie, sheer magic."

Which, in Josie's estimation, made it even worse.

She groaned and rested her forearm across her eyes. It didn't take a psychologist to know she should have used a lot more common sense. But with his arms around her and his lips on hers, it had been hard for her to think about anything but the tenderness of his touch, the utter deliciousness of his kisses and the reassuringly strong and warm and male feel of him. She had been looking for a man this wonderful all her life. Wouldn't it figure that she'd find the man of her dreams now, when she was least equipped to deal with him or the 100 percent honesty and forthrightness Wade required from the woman in his life?

Wade studied her. "It's our business relationship, isn't it?" he guessed wrongly.

Josie rolled onto her stomach, buried her face in her pillow and confirmed this was at least part of her current conflict with a low, anguished groan. Clamping her lips together, she shut her eyes, knowing on that level—of professional ethics—she did feel a very sharp, potent regret. Because she knew—even though she didn't actually regret doing so under the circumstances—that she had crossed a line that should never have been crossed in taking on the drilling of his well, in getting involved with him, in making love with him as if there was no tomorrow.

"You're a client of Wyatt Drilling," she pointed out miserably. And because of that—because she hadn't been honest with him from the start and because she had taken on Wade's business without the authority she needed—she should have waited before bringing sex and love and passion into the mix.

But Wade apparently didn't see it that way. Wade saw only what they had felt. Only what they had discovered in each other's hearts and souls and arms.

Wade kissed his way across her bare shoulders as his hands slid beneath her to cup her breasts. "Business had absolutely nothing to do with what just happened, Josie."

Ignoring the tingling of her nipples and, lower still, the butterflies of desire that began to build, Josie rolled over to face him once again. "But it should have," Josie said sternly, still trying to calm the racing of her heart and the renewed desire that was steadily building, deep inside her.

His eyes still on hers, Wade shook his head firmly. "No." He looked deep into her eyes. "Some things have nothing to do with business. The two of us making love is one of them."

Josie only hoped he would still feel that way later, when he put two and two together—as he no doubt would—and realized how and why she had kissed him when she had. So he wouldn't read the news about the South American oil strike.

Josie flushed with guilt, knowing that even though their lovemaking had come about because of what had been in her heart, that he might not see it that way when he found out all there was to be found out. "The kiss was impulsive," Josie said. She swallowed hard and forced herself to not only hold his gaze but be brutally honest about as much as possible. "And I'll be first to admit that I intended to give that kiss my full attention and a 100 percent effort." After all, she rationalized firmly, what was a mere kiss? It didn't carry anywhere near the import—or the inherent commitment—of actually making love. "But that was all I intended, Wade, when I launched myself into your arms," she whispered sincerely. "A simple kiss." Her reaction to the passion, her incredible need to make love to him, had been a total surprise.

"Don't you think I know that?" Wade whispered huskily against her throat, as his hands warmly cupped her breasts. "Don't you think I felt your surprise when the sparks took off and one kiss led to another and another? Trust me, Josie. There was no way I could miss the heat of your body and the quick intake of your breath, the way your nipples pebbled against my hands or the way your thighs draped mine—even before I made you mine. Any more than you could miss the quickening of my heart or the throbbing hardness here." He pressed her hand to him.

"So we wanted each other," Josie breathed, luxuriating in the warm, velvety feel of his erection beneath her palm. An erection she hadn't had nearly enough time or opportunity to explore.

"Still want each other," Wade corrected, bathing her nipples with his lips and tongue until she arched against him wantonly and threaded both hands through his hair.

Josie closed her eyes against the wildfire of sensations flowing through her and the near incessant need to make love with him again. "That's still no excuse for my behavior," she moaned. Especially the way she had deceived him from the very first fax.

Upset with herself over the duplicity that might one day soon prove their undoing, and wrench Wade from her life forever, she pushed away from him and vaulted from the bed. Wrapping a sheet around her, she rushed into the adjacent bathroom.

"You're right. It isn't," he growled, striding after her. Backing her up against the bathroom counter, he tugged her against his nakedness, until there was no doubting, no ignoring, his considerable arousal. "And you know why?" He separated the edges of the sheet, parted her thighs with his knee and moved in to partake of her heat. "Because we don't need an excuse." Hands on her hips, Wade guided her closer, fitting softness to hardness. "We're adults, Josie." His hands caressed her shoulders, moved tenderly over the bare skin of her back. "Wise in the ways of the world if not each other, yet. But we can fix that, too." His hands skimmed up over her sides, her ribs. He gently cupped the weight of both her breasts with his palms and bent to kiss her sweetly. "All it's going to take is a little more practice and a little time."

He kissed her hotly, until Josie trembled and her knees went weak. He stroked her dewy softness, moving up, in. Aware she could barely stand, even with his help, Josie clung to him and whispered, "I can't believe you're—it's only been—"

"Tell me about it." Wade grinned triumphantly, all sexy possessive male. He opened the glass shower door and waltzed her backward into the shower stall. He turned on the water.

It was cold at first, then gradually warmer. But nothing compared to his deep, passionate kisses or the heat in his eyes, Josie thought. Nothing compared to the wonderfully womanly way he made her feel. "Wade," she whispered, knowing even as she spoke she would never get enough of him.

"Let me love you, Josie," Wade whispered as he began to make mad, passionate love to her all over again. Commanding everything she had to give and giving her everything in return. Loving…needing…her with every fiber of his being. "Just let me love you."

"Problem?" Josie asked an hour and a half later as Wade hung up the phone.

"Big one." Wade confirmed as he watched Josie remove her last load of clothes from his dryer.

After their last bout of incredibly passionate, incredibly wonderful lovemaking, the two of them had decided to stop worrying about the possible impropriety of their relationship and take it one day—one moment—at a time. It was an agreement Josie found she could live with. Complications aside, she wanted to continue their affair. She didn't want any strings. Not until they'd struck oil, anyway, and she could straighten things out with her father and mother, once and for all.

The moment she got herself out of this mess that she'd gotten herself in, she would go to Wade and tell him everything. She just hoped he would understand why she had behaved as recklessly as she had and forgive her for not leveling with him from the very beginning.

Wade wrapped his arms about her shoulders and coaxed her into the warm curve of his body. "The messenger service just delivered a big box with my name on it over at the Laramie Community Center."

Josie folded her clothes quickly, stuffing them into

the top of the laundry bag as soon as they were folded. "Do you know what it is?"

Wade tugged her closer yet and pressed tiny kisses into her hair. "The architectural model of the new wing for the hospital. It was supposed to come here, not there."

Finished, Josie turned to face him. "You're afraid someone will see it and tell your folks there's a big package over there with your name on it?"

Wade nodded. He urged her closer with the flat of his hand. Their bodies fit together like a lock and key. She could feel his arousal, and recalled all too vividly what a demanding and yet ultimately giving lover he had been. "You got it. If that were to happen, they'd know something was up—so I've got to go right over and get it."

He was talking to her so intimately and looking at her with so much tenderness. If she didn't know better, she would think he was desperately in love with her.

"Fortunately," Wade continued gently, "the secretary said there is nothing going on there between 5:00 and 6:00 p.m., so we can get it then and have a look around, too. You can see where the party for my folks is going to be held and figure out if there's anything we forgot to arrange today."

Just that quickly he had included her in his life. Josie tried not to think how good that felt. Or how bereft she would feel if he pushed her out of it again. "Presuming a lot, aren't you, cowboy?" Josie teased.

"Hoping." Wade kissed her cheek. "And you're darn right—I am."

They drove over to the rec center, arriving just as the

center secretary was getting ready to leave for the day. "Take as much time as you need looking around." She handed Wade the keys to the storeroom—where the box was located. "Just lock up and put the storeroom keys in my desk drawer before you leave."

"I don't know about you, but I can't wait to get a look at the architectural model," Wade said.

Josie smiled at Wade. He had shaved again after they'd made love in the shower, and his jaw was scented with the enticing fragrance of sandalwood and leather. "You haven't seen it yet?" she asked. He looked so handsome in his camel-colored Western sport coat, light blue Western shirt and jeans.

"Only sketches." Wade borrowed the letter opener on the secretary's desk. He sliced through the brown tape that sealed the edges. Together, they removed the packing material around the model and lifted it ever so carefully out of the box.

Josie looked at the model of the new wing, which was built in the same turn-of-the-century Texas design as the rest of the hospital. It was obvious a lot of thought and care had gone into this project, from the design of the long narrow windows and the plentiful landscaping and new three-tiered parking garage to the seamless way the new wing merged with the rest of the historic building. "It's beautiful," she said. And it was a very generous, very selfless thing for him to do.

Wade sighed in satisfaction as she looked over the model carefully. "I think my parents are really going to like it," he told her proudly.

"And so will the rest of the community."

Without warning, a door shut in the distance.

As the soft thudding sound reverberated in the still-
ness, Josie looked at Wade curiously. "I thought we
were supposed to be the only two people here right
now."

"We are." Grimacing, Wade got up to quickly shut
the storeroom door and thereby block off the model of
the new hospital wing from view.

Catching sight of the interlopers, he swore softly beneath his breath.

"Who is it?" Josie whispered, as he peered around
the door frame.

Wade closed the door as soundlessly as possible and
put a silencing finger to his lips. "Don't say a word," he
mouthed. And a second later Josie knew why.

Chapter 9

"He's not here." John McCabe's deep baritone echoed through the empty rec center.

"Then I'd like to know where that son of ours is," Lilah McCabe countered in obvious vexation. "That's his Ford Expedition in the parking lot."

Beside her, Josie felt Wade tense. But there was nothing they could do unless they wanted to reveal themselves and ruin the surprise for his parents.

"He could be anywhere in the downtown area," John countered, sounding ready to wrap it up.

"And why is this building unlocked if no one is here?" Lilah demanded, her purposeful footsteps moving past the storeroom with lightning speed.

"You're asking the wrong person, dear."

"I'm worried about him, John," Lilah stated passionately, as Wade's tall, strong body tensed all the more.

"Wade's fine."

"But he's not happy," Lilah persisted emotionally. "I know he's not."

John sighed. "Give him time."

"I have. We both have. And he still doesn't know how to let someone get close to him." Lilah paused, then continued, even more emotionally, "We never should have let him start earning all that money at such an early age."

"Do you really think we could have stopped him?" John McCabe retorted, just as passionately. "Delayed it, maybe. But stopped him? Honey, people with Wade's kind of talent for making money end up like Donald Trump as surely as you and I ended up being healers and working in the medical profession."

"But the money, John, all that money!" Lilah worried out loud. "All it does is serve to keep people away from him."

Isn't that the truth, Josie thought, knowing how many friendships and opportunities had been denied her when people learned she had a trust fund.

"It isn't the money keeping people at arm's length, Lilah. It's him. Until he learns to open up—to trust someone enough to confide in them—then there's no way he's ever gonna get married," John retorted sternly.

"I know, I know." Lilah sighed tiredly. "I just want all of our boys happy."

"And they will be, Lilah," John McCabe soothed lovingly. "Just give them time."

The voices faded away. The front door to the rec center shut. For a moment Wade and Josie were both motionless, then Wade reached over and switched on the storeroom light. His face looked strained in the fluorescent light.

"I'm sorry I heard that," Josie said, her heart going out to him. She knew it had embarrassed—and hurt—him. Worse, she knew how it felt. Her parents often despaired over her and her life in much the same way.

Wade shrugged. Faint streaks of color stained his face from cheekbone to jaw. "It's okay. I'm used to it. The assumption within the family—and outside it—has always been that because I'm so good at making money I have very little heart." He paused and looked deep into her eyes as if trying to be understood.

"Sort of goes with being so rich at such a young age, I guess." He paused, a brooding expression on his face, a distant look in his eyes. He turned away again. "The sad thing is—as much as I hate to admit it—my parents are right." His sensual mouth tightened into a self-effacing line. "Keeping people at arm's length is comfortable for me. That's why I dated all the shallow debs—because they had no interest in getting to know the real me as long as I showed them a good time, took them to the best nightspots and picked up the check."

Josie understood. Since the demise of her engagement to Ben, she had purposefully selected escorts who would not make any demands on her. Escorts who were all too willing to accompany her to and from foundation or charity events, but were not looking for a soul mate or life partner or anything else she was unable or unwilling to give. Which, in the final analysis, usually left her with the emotional equivalent of having just dated an inflatable Safety Man doll. Which, oddly enough, had been just fine with her.

Wade frowned. "Being vulnerable to someone else isn't comfortable. And yet I know the only way you can get really close to someone is by letting your guard down and opening up your heart. For instance, if there was something you needed or wanted to tell me, even if it was something really bad or embarrassing or private, then you should be able to do so, just like that." He snapped his fingers.

Josie only wished that were the case.

He continued to study her, eventually guessing somewhat dejectedly, "But you can't confide in me like that, can you?"

Josie wanted to tell him everything, but she couldn't. Not yet. But soon, hopefully. She swallowed, doing her best not to hurt him and still be as honest as possible. "We're getting closer."

"Right." Hurt shimmering in his eyes, he turned away.

She couldn't bear the disappointment she'd seen on his face.

"Wade—" She caught him by the arm, her fingers curling around the strength and warmth of his bicep.

He turned, an expectant look in his eyes.

"You're not the only one who has shortcomings," Josie confessed softly, studying the tortured expression on his handsome face. "I struggle with mine, too." She swallowed. "It doesn't mean we should give up on us," she continued passionately. "Heck, we're just getting started."

"You're right." He hooked an arm about her waist. "We are." He traced the curve of her cheek with the side of his hand. "I shouldn't push it. But—as with everything else in my life—I want what I want when I want it." He gathered her to him for a searing kiss. Josie wrapped her arms around him, gave in to the feelings that had been building and met him, caress for caress. By the time the languid kiss came to an end, both of them were trembling. And yearning to do more.

Aware this was neither the time nor the place for an interlude, Josie hitched a breath in. "We better get out of here," she said shakily.

"You're right," he said softly, affectionately, tracing her face with his hand. "We should." Ever so reluctantly, they moved apart.

Wade picked up the box. Josie opened the door to the storeroom. And both came face-to-face with Lilah and John McCabe.

"See?" Lilah McCabe elbowed her husband John decisively. "I told you it was worth coming back for one last look."

John McCabe looked at both Josie and Wade. Never one to pussyfoot around, he got straight to the point. "What are you two doing here?"

"And what's in the box?" Lilah added.

Keeping his face expressionless, Wade set it down. Ever so casually, he fibbed. "The box contains a gift for your getting-married-all-over-again-shower on Saturday night. It was mistakenly delivered here. The rec center secretary called me to come pick it up."

"Mmm-hmm." Lilah looked at both of them, then zeroed in on her son. "I know that too-innocent look, Wade McCabe. You're up to something. What's going on here?"

Josie swallowed nervously and turned to Wade. Wade looked at Josie's flushed, upturned face. Wade knew he was going to have to come up with something. Fast. Or the surprise for his folks really would be ruined.

Still looking at Josie, Wade shrugged. "We might as well tell them."

Josie gulped again. "Are you sure?"

Wade squeezed her hand and turned back to his folks, determined to tell as much of the truth as he could. "I want Josie to go with me to the big party here on Friday night. She hasn't said yes yet," he amended hastily as Josie tensed in surprise.

"Why not?" Lilah cut in, looking at Josie.

Josie turned to Wade. "You tell them," she said oh, so sweetly, giving him a dire look only he could see.

Sensing Josie was about to bolt, Wade clamped his hands possessively on her shoulders. And, in an effort to calm her, caressed them reassuringly. "Josie's not really at ease in situations where she has to act all ladylike and everything," he said. His eyes glimmering with barely checked humor, he continued with exaggerated solemnness. "She's a lady roughneck, you know," Wade drawled as Josie's eyes widened in surprise. "And that's why we're here."

Lilah blinked, confused. "I don't understand."

Wade looked at Josie, mischief only she could see sparkling in his eyes. He continued to provide cover for them, preserve the surprise for his folks and tease her mercilessly all at the same time. "We might as well tell them everything that's been going on between us, sweetheart, and get 'em up to speed."

Everything? Josie thought, aghast. And let his parents know they'd made love?

Blushing fiercely, Josie clutched his arm. "Wade," she warned, ever so deliberately. "I know what you're saying but I don't think—"

Wade laced his arm comfortingly about her shoulders and patted her arm. "It's okay, hon. They'll understand. Josie asked me—well, actually I volunteered—to teach her how to be a lady. I've dated a lot of debs, so I figure, who would know better, right?"

Wade's mother straightened the hem of her pink cardigan with a sigh. "Oh, Wade, not again!" Lilah said.

"Not again what?" Josie asked, turning back to Lilah.

John sighed. "Wade tries to make over all the women he dates to suit him. To the point his brothers have joked what he really wants is a Stepford wife, Laramie style."

"Cooking, dressing, behaving, goals. Before all is said and done Wade meddles in every aspect of his girlfriends' lives, no matter how often we tell him not to do it!" Lilah sighed. Then continued with a firm look at her son, "He has to learn if he loves a woman he loves her for who and what she is, not with an eye to transforming her into something else."

"In the meantime, feel free to kick his shin anytime you want," John McCabe told Josie.

Josie, whose worst fear was being abandoned because she somehow didn't measure up to someone else's expectations of her, glowered at Wade, then turned back to John. Was this what she was getting herself into? More unhappiness on the romance front? Initially she'd thought Wade was just acting that way to get her attention. But if this was a pattern, that was something else indeed.

Josie turned back to John. "I just might take you up on that," she demurred. Certainly the idea of teaching the sometimes-overbearing Wade a lesson or two appealed to the feminine side of her.

"Excuse me, you two," Wade interrupted his dad and Josie, forcefully enough to completely divert everyone's attention from the box. "We're trying to have a discussion here. So you should stay on topic. Now, back to this being-a-lady stuff. First and foremost, at any big party, is knowing how to dance. Josie, sad to say, sometimes has a little trouble staying with the beat of the music. Not to mention a little trouble walking like a lady."

Completely exasperated with him by now, Josie rolled her eyes.

Ignoring her, Wade continued his much-too-lengthy, much-too-detailed explanation. "As long as I had to come over here to get the package, I suggested we try dancing on this floor. Sort of a trial run." He spread his hands wide. "Only I forgot to bring my stereo and she doesn't like my singing."

"Or your storytelling," Josie cut in.

Wade gave her a quelling look, then turned back to his parents. "So we went looking for a stereo. Couldn't find one. Decided to give up and just practice some more later, at her trailer or my ranch house, and then we went to get the package."

"Hasn't anyone ever told you less is more?" Josie cut in dryly. "Your parents probably don't need—or want—to know all that," she told Wade meaningfully.

Wade turned and looked deep into Josie's eyes. While Lilah looked at her son with barely masked exasperation. It didn't take a rocket scientist to figure out that Lilah McCabe knew full well her son wasn't telling her everything. "You really expect me to believe all this?" Lilah questioned dryly, propping her hands on her hips.

"It's true, isn't it, Josie?" Wade turned to look at her. He held her eyes with a look that was all innocence. He didn't like misleading his folks, the tiniest bit, even for a good reason. On the other hand, he didn't want them nosing around in his love affair with Josie, either. "I have been giving you dancing lessons." He telegraphed the need for her continued cooperation with a look.

"One," Josie corrected sweetly. And it took every ounce of self-restraint Wade possessed to keep from taking her into his arms and kissing her madly.

"You've given me one dancing lesson," Josie corrected. "So far, anyway," she added sweetly.

And he wanted to give her many more lessons in the art of kissing and making love, Wade thought. Not because Josie needed them. Heck, she was a great kisser. And even better at making love. No, he wanted to make love to her again because he was in love with her. And soon she'd know it, too, Wade thought. But right now he had to deal with his parents.

"I stand corrected. One lesson," Wade said, his hot glance skimming her from head to toe. "So—" he placed a proprietary arm around Josie's waist and looked at his parents cheerfully "—as you can see, Josie and I've got our work cut out for us if we're going to be dancing together at the big bash here on Friday night."

Especially since he had apparently ticked her off by revealing the dancing lesson.

John looked at Josie. "I hope you'll be there. It should prove to be a fun evening."

"Did Wade tell you it's black tie?" Lilah put in helpfully, beginning to look a little worried at the continued tension between Wade and Josie. "So if you need to get a dress for the event, I could probably help you with that."

Wade added enthusiastically, "Josie's mama in Dallas sent her a real pretty dress to wear. As I said, Josie has a little trouble looking feminine sometimes, so I'm hoping—if we work on her dancing a little more and I buy her a real pretty pair of boots—that she'll go with me on Friday night. So what do you say, Josie?" Wade prodded, loving the excited blush of color that had come into her cheeks almost as much as the glitter in her eyes that told him she would not allow him to have the upper hand in their relationship. Not now. Not ever.

"Will you go with me?" he asked softly, aware of the irony of asking Josie for a first official date after they'd already spent the afternoon making mad, passionate love. He already felt as if she was his woman and would be for the rest of his life. He hadn't, however, done much courting, Wade realized guiltily. And that was something that was going to have to be rectified. Pronto. A woman as wonderful as Josie deserved a lot of courting. He took her by the hand and got down on bended knee. Looking up at her, with all the affection he felt for her reflected in his eyes, he asked softly, meaningfully, "Will you be my girl?"

* * *

"I can't believe you did that!" Josie fumed, the minute Lilah and John had departed the rec center. She looked grievously affronted! Probably, Wade thought, because she felt it had all been for show. It hadn't. But convincing her of that now, he realized with regret, was probably just not going to be possible. He'd have to do it later, when her temper had abated and they were alone. And he could show her—through kiss and touch—how he felt about her, how very much he cared.

Wade shrugged his broad shoulders affably. "I had to throw my parents off the track somehow so their surprise wouldn't be spoiled. Not that I mind—" Wade winked at her, aware they were so close they were touching "—since you agreed to be my date Friday night."

"What choice did I have but to agree?" Josie volleyed back, more emotionally than ever. She propped her clenched fists on her slender hips and tilted her chin up to his. "I had to shut you up somehow!" she stormed.

Wade grinned. "You could have tried this!" he said. He planted one hand at the base of her spine, the other at her nape. Hauling her close, he dipped his head and delivered a searing kiss. With a low moan of satisfaction Wade threaded his hand through the hair at the back of her neck and angled her head so their kiss could deepen. His other hand pressed against her spine, drawing her closer, until her breasts were pressed against his chest. She murmured her acquiescence in a soft sigh. Wade shuddered as her tongue swept his mouth, hotly and voraciously, and her muscles—tense and strained only moments before—quickly molded to him. Her heart was pounding in a trip-hammer rhythm that matched his. As they continued to kiss, her mouth contoured gently to his, she arched against him wantonly, as if she—like he—wanted this never to end. And it was that reaction, plus the knowledge of the place they were in, that forced Wade to end the kiss. He would finish this, he thought, releasing her ever so slowly and reluctantly. But it would be later, when he could give her all the time and attention she needed.

Breathless and disheveled, Josie pulled back. Her blue eyes shimmering with an unmistakably aroused light, she looked up at him and shook her head. "You are so bad."

"And bound to get more wickedly mischievous still," Wade promised, pulling her closer for one last, loving kiss that soon had them both trembling and wishing for more.

"Now, let's go get you fitted for those boots."

Josie blinked as she blotted the moisture from her lips and tried to restore some semblance of order to her hair. "You weren't serious about that," she exclaimed dryly.

Wade liked her like that—all soft and disheveled and ready to jump back in his waiting arms. He put an arm around her shoulders and drew her intimately close.

If this was what it was like after keeping company with her only a couple of days, how would he feel after a week or two. He was already counting the minutes whenever they were apart, whereas time just flew by when they were together. Wade figured this must be what it was like when you were falling in love in a way that would last your whole life through. It must be what his parents had felt when they got together, and what they still felt. And perhaps why they wanted it for him so much.

Suddenly the idea of getting married and having kids didn't seem as though it was something he ought to be running from. Especially with Josie in his life. "Josie, honey, when it comes to pampering my woman and making sure she has the best this life has to offer, I am always serious."

Judging from the look on Josie's face, she liked the sound of that. Wade smiled. So did he.

By the time they stopped by the boot makers, it was past seven. "You sure you don't want to stay in town and grab some dinner?" Wade asked.

Josie shook her head, her guilt over having been away from the drilling site most of the day increasing by leaps and bounds. "I've really got to get back, Wade. I never meant to be gone this long as it is."

During the twenty miles back to the Golden Slipper Ranch, Josie and Wade talked about the party. To Wade's delight, Josie was almost as excited as he was about the upcoming event. But all that changed when Josie saw the big white Cadillac parked in front of her trailer with the license plate reading BITSYC.

Wade tracked the hot flush of mortification spreading across Josie's face. "Someone you know?"

"It's my mother," Josie mumbled, looking all the more embarrassed. "I should have known she'd show up here in person to try to convince me to go back to Dallas."

Wade recalled Meg Lockhart's warning to Josie, earlier in the week. "Just tell her it's not that simple—that you've got a life going on here."

She sure did have a life going on here, Josie thought. With Wade. Not that this would make a difference to Bitsy, who was determined to get her as far away from the oil fields as possible. "To her, it is that simple," Josie replied flatly as she unhooked her seat belt. Contemplating the task ahead, she moaned and pushed both hands through her hair.

"Let me go in with you," Wade said.

"No," Josie replied quickly. She didn't want Bitsy carrying on in front of him. She put up both hands to ward off his help. "I really need to handle her alone. Please."

"You're sure?" Wade frowned, looking unhappier—and more protective of Josie—still.

"I promise. You can meet her some other time. Just not yet."

Bitsy started in on Josie the moment Josie stepped inside her trailer. "I can't believe you're using your trust fund to pay for this—this lunacy!"

"I'm loaning myself the money. Wade McCabe will reimburse me for any costs I incur once we strike oil on the Golden Slipper."

"And what if you don't? What then?" Bitsy voiced Josie's worst fear.

Josie drew a breath and faced the petite, dark-haired woman she loved more than life itself but could never ever seem to please.

With a beleaguered sigh, Josie sat down at the kitchen table. Her own jeans, faded yellow T-shirt and dusty boots in direct contrast with her mother's azalea-red silk couture pantsuit and matching shoes. Diamonds sparkled in her earlobes and on both manicured hands. Her delicate, expertly made-up features were framed by a stylish short cut, and not a hair was out of place. But even though Bitsy looked like she spent twenty-four hours of the day just getting beautiful, Josie knew nothing was further from the truth. Bitsy could be in and out of the bath in under an hour. She spent long hours running the family foundation, and even longer hours raising additional funds for the various charities the Corbett Foundation supported. She was a beautiful, dynamic, popular, successful Wonder Woman. Next to her Josie always felt like a pale imitation. But that wasn't her mother's fault, Josie knew. It was because she hadn't proved herself yet. Once she had, everything would change.

Josie leaned forward, elbows on the table, hands clasped loosely in front of her. "Mom, there's oil here. I can feel it in my bones."

Bitsy released an aggravated breath. "Not that again!" Bitsy's delicate lips pursed. "I declare I'm going to wring your father's neck for encouraging you all these years!"

Josie pushed away from the table and began to pace, restlessness overtaking her once again. She flattened her hands on the back of her waist and stared out the window at the drilling rig in the distance. "Big Jim never encouraged me to be a wildcatter, Mom. You know that," Josie reminded tiredly.

Her mother stomped nearer, the spike heels of her designer shoes making a staccato sound across the mud-tracked linoleum floor. Bitsy looked askance at the dirty dishes Josie had left in the sink that morning. Josie thought about explaining that she didn't have servants here to help her as her mother did in Dallas—nor did she want any—it had been raining that morning, and there had been trouble on the rig when she had rushed out to help, and she'd been gone all day and would have cleaned up that evening in any case. But it didn't seem to matter. She didn't have to hear a word to know Bitsy disapproved of the path she had chosen.

"But he did challenge you to figure out where oil was located and where it wasn't," Bitsy pointed out.

Josie threw up her hands in exasperation. "It was a game we played when I was a kid!" Scowling, she picked up the roll of paper towels and the spray bottle of kitchen cleaner and went to work on the muddy floor. "He did it to keep me occupied and interested in what was going on, whenever I was with him." And she'd had a blast doing it!

Bitsy shook her head as Josie squirted cleaner on all the footprints. "I knew nothing good could come of Jim dragging you to all those drilling sites," Bitsy fumed.

Josie tore off squares of paper towels and put them over the cleaner-drenched spots. "Mom, I know you don't like it, but wildcatting is what I was born to do."

"Josie, be reasonable. Think of your future!"

"I am!" Josie used the sole of her boots to drag the paper towels across the floor, soaking up mud and cleaner all the while. "I'm trying to build a future for myself."

Bitsy stepped back to clear the way for Josie to slide-

and-clean the rest of the floor. "Your future is the foundation."

"No, Mom," Josie sprayed cleaner on the spots she had missed, "the foundation is your thing, and I'm happy it is. But it's not mine," Josie said gently. She tore off more towels.

Bitsy scowled as she watched Josie toss down more paper toweling. "Then find something else," she instructed emotionally.

"I have."

"Something ladylike."

"I don't want to do something ladylike." Her boot-clad feet on separate towels, Josie skated her way across the floor, awkwardly slip-sliding and cleaning as she went. "I am sick to death of doing ladylike things."

"Josie, for heaven's sake!" Bitsy finally blew up. "Who in their right mind is going to want to marry a lady roughneck, never mind even date one?"

"I will."

Josie and Bitsy turned in unison. Wade was framed in the doorway. He had Josie's battered leather shoulder bag in his hands. He tipped the brim of his hat at them both. "Didn't mean to overhear or interrupt, ladies, but you forgot this."

Bitsy blinked. Wade touched the brim of his hat once again. "Wade McCabe, ma'am. At your service."

Bitsy scowled and propped her beringed hands on her hips. "Don't tell me you're encouraging my daughter, too?" she remarked icily.

Wade stepped inside. He handed Josie her bag—which she set on the table—then hunkered down beside her to help her retrieve the soggy paper towels scattered across the floor. "As it happens," Wade drawled, pausing to toss the first of a dozen paper towels into the trash, "having seen Josie in action around the site, yeah, you might say I'm encouraging her. And with good reason." Wade looked Bitsy square in the eye. "She really knows her stuff. And if you want my opinion," Wade and Josie picked up the rest of the grungy towels, "Josie ought to be respected for that, instead of put down." Finished, Wade stood and gave Josie a hand up.

Bitsy continued to study Wade for a long silent moment, cataloguing his six-foot-five, two-hundred-twenty-pound frame. Wordlessly she assessed the superb fit and quality of his camel-colored Western sport coat, light blue Western shirt, jeans and hand-tooled Western boots. Took in the rumpled layers of his ash brown hair, his ruggedly handsome features and dark brown eyes, his straight blade nose and sensually chiseled lips.

And when all that met her exceedingly high standards, as Josie could see it did, Bitsy began to concentrate on what was in Wade McCabe's heart and soul and eyes. "No one is going to marry her, Mr. McCabe, if she continues in this vein," Bitsy continued in her soft, worried voice.

Josie tensed, wondering what Wade would say to that. She didn't have to wait long to find out. He took off his hat, dropped it on the table, shrugged out of his sport coat and hung that over the back of a chair. Looking much more at home, he reached out and laced an arm around Josie's waist and reeled her in to his side.

"Any man worth marrying would accept Josie's choice of career, no matter what it is," Wade returned bluntly. He turned to Josie and regarded her lovingly. "I wouldn't expect or want you to settle for anything less. And frankly, neither should your loved ones."

The warmth and affection in his eyes made Josie's knees go weak.

"Well." Bitsy splayed a hand over her heart. "You certainly have no trouble speaking your mind, do you, Mr. McCabe?"

"I'm just defending my…friend. No disrespect meant," Wade told Bitsy courteously, reaching past Josie to shake Bitsy's hand.

"None taken," Bitsy murmured back, looking intrigued—and yes, pleased—by Josie's choice of companion. It was all Josie could do not to groan. The last thing she wanted was Bitsy championing her relationship with Wade. She didn't want Bitsy—or Big Jim—involved in her personal life at all.

Trying her best to prevent any more tension, Josie cut in politely. "Mom, maybe this isn't the best time to discuss private family matters." Especially financial ones, she thought nervously, her mind going back to her trust fund.

Bitsy glanced at her watch, frowned as she noted the time. Already reaching for her designer handbag and car keys, she turned back to Josie. "Don't think for one minute that we're finished talking about this, because we are not. But unfortunately I've got a previous engagement."

Bitsy said a brief goodbye and rushed out.

Silence fell.

As soon as Bitsy's Cadillac drove off, Josie let out a long, relieved breath. Aware Wade still had his hand locked around her waist, Josie thought about how good it had felt to allow him to come to her rescue like that. "Thanks." Josie's hands were trembling. She felt like bursting into tears. She went to get herself a glass of water. She leaned against the sink and took a thirsty gulp. "I don't know why I let her get to me like that."

"If you want to talk about it," Wade said gently, "I'd be more than happy to listen."

As she looked at the compassion in Wade's eyes, Josie realized she needed to unburden herself. She got glasses of ice water for them both, took his hand and led him over to the sofa, where she settled in the curve of his arm. "I don't know any of the details of how my parents met or ever got together because both steadfastly refuse to talk about it, except to say they had a very intense, very passionate fling that led to her getting pregnant. But I do know my parents never should have married." Josie paused and shook her head.

"My dad was a roughneck from the wrong side of the tracks whose only real love is wildcatting. My mother was from the right side of the tracks and she has great social aspirations—not just for herself but for me, too."

Pain colored Josie's low voice as she continued to remember, "Neither my mom nor my dad ever lived up to each other's expectations. She wasn't the wife he needed. He wasn't the husband she needed. So they cut each other out of their lives—literally—before I was even born, separating while my mother was still pregnant with me and divorcing a suitable time after."

Wade lifted her hand to his lips and kissed the back

of it tenderly. "That must have been rough. Although, under the circumstances, maybe it was a good thing they did end their marriage."

"You're right." Josie rested the back of her head on Wade's shoulder. She had never felt this safe or secure. "Like oil and water, the two of them will never mix. They've both told me many times that passion alone is not enough to sustain a marriage. You have to have similar views, backgrounds, aspirations if you want to have a relationship that lasts a lifetime."

"I'm not sure I agree about that." Wade turned slightly to face her, the hardness of his thigh pressing up against hers. He traced a lazy pattern on her knee. "What is it they say about opposites attracting?" he teased.

Josie's lips took on a rueful curve. Once again, she didn't know whether to laugh or cry. She only knew she didn't want to live through the kind of tempestuous, unhappy relationship her parents had forged for themselves. "You wouldn't say that if you'd had the kind of childhood I had," she pointed out sagely.

Wade rubbed her palm between the two of his. "Rough?"

"And then some." For a moment Josie luxuriated in the feel of his warm, callused hands massaging her skin. She bit her lip. "I knew they both loved me. But I've never stopped feeling torn between the two."

Josie paused and looked deep into Wade's eyes. "The truth is they're warring factions even now. My mother wants me to wear beautiful clothing and look and act like a proper Southern lady at all times. She also wants me to have a high-powered white-collar career. My father wants me to forget that world and be an exceedingly practical woman who spends the majority of her time supporting her husband's career."

Wade made a face. "I can see where that would have been confusing when you were younger," he said dryly.

"The worst part is I don't think either of them are willing to accept me or see me for who I am. Even now." Feeling tears of frustration and hurt fill her eyes, Josie shrugged and willed the tears not to fall. "Not that I've got it all figured out quite yet," she confessed thickly. "If I had, I wouldn't be opting for a career and life-style change at this point in my life."

Wade grinned as he continued rubbing Josie's hand, until the rest of her felt as relaxed as her palm. "There's plenty of time for you and me both to figure out what we want to do with all aspects of our lives."

That was true, Josie thought.

He paused and studied her face. "Something else is still bothering you," he guessed.

Josie shrugged. "You saw the way my mother reacted just now. My dad's been every bit as unsupportive. I'm afraid if I'm not the daughter both of them need, want and expect, that they will stop loving me, the same way they stopped loving each other years ago."

"Hey," Wade said hurriedly. "That's not going to happen." He took her all the way into his arms.

Josie hitched in a breath even as she relaxed against him. She looked up into his face. "How do you know?"

Wade stroked a hand through the silk of Josie's hair. He loved the way she felt all snuggled up beside him.

"Because I know you," he told her gently, wanting more than anything to reassure her. "And I know what a special woman you are. Your parents would have to be crazy not to want you in their lives. They might be demanding, but they're not crazy." Wade turned her, so her back was to him. He put both hands on her shoulders and massaged them gently. "Besides—" he leaned forward and kissed the top of her head "—no one ever said you couldn't wear a lot of different hats and look good in them all."

Josie glanced at him over her shoulder. She furrowed her brow.

"What do you mean?"

"You can be a tomboy slash wildcatter one day, a femme fatale slash city girl the next. And look terrific and be perfectly happy in both roles." As Wade continued massaging her shoulders, he felt some of the tension leave her.

Josie sighed happily and shut her eyes. She let her head fall back. "You're good for my ego, you know that?"

Wade smiled. There was so much more he could do for her. "I hope I'm good for a lot more than that."

At the sexual undertone in his voice, Josie turned. "Wade…" she chided sternly. But there was a new and ardent excitement glimmering in her azure-blue eyes.

"I drove over to the drilling rig to get an update while you were talking to your mom. The drill-stem test won't be completed for another two hours. There's nothing for you to do over there except wait and pace, so Gus, Ernie and Dieter told you to stay put. They'll call you when the test results are in, and you can go over then. Meantime—" Wade rolled to his feet. He offered Josie a hand and helped her up.

Color flooded her cheeks as she began to see where this was headed. Josie's mouth opened in surprise. "You're not suggesting," she said in a low, shocked voice.

"Yes, Josie, I am." Wade tunneled both hands through her hair and bent to kiss her tenderly. He knew she was used to thinking in terms of work first. So was he. But there were times when it was necessary to put work aside. This was one of them. "I want some time with you, too. And you can be as much a proper Southern lady in my arms as you want," he teased huskily as he swept her up into his arms, carried her into the bedroom at the rear of her trailer and set her down beside the bed. "I won't tell a soul."

Josie's legs trembled as much as the rest of her. She gave him an arch look and stepped back as much as his hands would allow. "I never said I wanted to be a proper Southern lady," she reminded coolly, tossing her head and stalking from him.

Amused by her display of temper, Wade hooked a hand in the waistband of her jeans and hauled her back to him. Josie was still a mystery to him in so many ways. But if he had his way she wouldn't be for much longer. "Then what do you want to be?" he demanded huskily. Hands gently caressing her shoulders, he turned her around to face him.

Josie sighed wistfully and looked up at him as if the answer to that was an easy one. "The kind of woman who doesn't worry as much about how she looks or what she wears, so much as what is in her heart." Josie's lips curved. "The kind of woman who's as at home on a drilling rig as she is at some fancy party. The kind who doesn't have to apologize about wearing jeans and boots 99 percent of the time."

Wade looked down at her fondly. Sliding both hands through her hair, he tilted her face up to his. As he studied her, his heart filled with tenderness and warmth. "Still a tomboy at heart, hmm?" he teased, loving the way she looked, with color in her cheeks and fire in her eyes.

Josie's breath caught in her chest, lifting the soft swell of her breasts. "And I always will be," Josie admitted recklessly as her fingers traced provocative patterns on the fabric of his shirt. "So you're going to have to give up on teaching me how to be a lady, Wade. And you're going to have to give up wishing I were free of flaws, because I'm just not," she finished ruefully, her arms tightening around him, strengthening, even as every bone in her body seemed to melt.

His need for her increasing, Wade tangled his fingers in her hair and touched his lips to hers. Gently and evocatively at first, then slowly and lingeringly. Until the tension between them began to abate, replaced by something infinitely sweeter and harder to curtail. Eyes still locked playfully with hers, he drew back. As always, Josie was much harder on herself than he thought she should be. And he wished—hoped—it would stop. "That's fine," he murmured teasingly as he gently tugged at a lock of her hair. Lacing his arms about her waist, he sat on the bed and shifted her closer, so she was standing between the open vee of his legs, the outside of her thighs pressed against the inside of his. "As long as I can teach you other things."

He looked up at her and felt himself lost in her, in love with her. Not just for today, but for all time. And yet, no matter how reckless and headstrong she was, no matter how daring or passionate, she was still the innocent in so many ways. And for that he had to be careful. Not to push too hard or too fast. Not to overwhelm her with confessions of his feelings for her. Confessions she could conclude were meant only to get her into bed.

No, the words would come—later—when she knew him well enough to trust that everything he said was true. And enduring. For now, he would show her how he felt. With touch and tenderness and need.

Josie's breath caught again as his hands skimmed down her body, his fingers brushing down the sides of her breasts, moving across her tummy, his palms cupping her waist, her hips, her thighs, before beginning the foray up, stroking and kneading, until the yearning ache grew and spread inside her. Her arms were wreathed around his shoulders, her heart pounding, as he began to unbuckle her belt and unzip her fly. Trying not to let him know how much he was affecting her, trying not to let him know how very much she loved him, for fear he'd think her even more reckless and impulsive when it came to getting what she wanted than she was, she lifted a dissenting brow. "You're never going to get over this got-to-improve-my-woman kick, are you?" she drawled.

"Realistically?" Lips curving in a seductive smile, he held her against him gently as he pushed her jeans to the floor and helped her step out of them. "Probably not." His hands hooked inside the elastic of her panties and pushed them down, too. "But the flip side of that is—" he pressed an all-too-brief, all-too-casual kiss to her navel, then divested her of her shirt and bra "—I'll let you improve on me, too." He rolled lazily to his feet. "And by the time we're done with each other, we'll both be better off."

Josie could think of a few things she'd like to do— like teach him to stop being so bossy and commanding. "Well, when you put it that way," she sighed contentedly as she helped him off with his shirt, jeans and shorts. Then placed both her arms about his neck and brought his head down to hers. "I guess I'm in."

"Good," Wade whispered, fitting his lips over hers. His arousal pressed against her, creating an ocean of warmth inside her. He shifted her closer, his tongue parting her lips, touching the edges of her teeth and then returning in a series of soft, drugging kisses that robbed her of the will and ability to think past the moment, the man and the desire flowing through her, more potent and mesmerizing than ever before. "Because I wouldn't want it any other way," Wade whispered, kissing her again and again and again.

When he laid her on the bed, she stirred languorously. He ran his hands over her body, covering it with kisses, learning her body, teaching her pleasure in ways she had never imagined. Needing to give, as well as receive, she let out a soft groan and rolled so that he was beneath her. Her lips and hands moved over his skin, luxuriating in the satiny warmth and strength of his chest and stomach and thighs. She couldn't get enough of touching him and kissing him, and that filled her with a kind of wonder, even as she settled over him, caressing the velvety length of him from tip to base. Whatever shyness she'd had, whatever fears and reservations, they were gone now. She wanted him deep inside her. She wanted tight sinew and taut flesh. She wanted tenderness and love. Soft kisses. Hard kisses. Kisses that fell in between. She got all that and more. From him. And she delivered all that and more. To him. Until she was shuddering and so was he, and all coherent thought spun away in frissons of endless pleasure.

"Now?" Wade murmured.

"Now," Josie agreed.

A wellspring of tenderness and need in his eyes, he moved over top of her, parting her thighs with his knee. Sliding his hands beneath her, he lifted her hips to his, surging slowly, deeply into her, into her life. She arched against him, her legs coming around him, drawing him deeper, giving him whatever he wanted, whatever he needed, whatever they both needed. Until they were gasping, shaking, drawn into a realm of sensation that had them both surging toward the outer limits of their control. How she needed this—how they both needed this—Josie thought as his fingers clamped onto hers. And holding tight, they soared into soft, sizzling love and shuddering pleasure.

Afterward Wade held her close. The pinnacle of pleasure had passed, leaving them exhausted and replete. And more than a little awed. Josie turned blindly into Wade's arms and buried her face in the soft hair on his chest. It would have been perfect, Josie thought wistfully, if not for the things Wade still didn't know. The closer they became, the harder it was going to be to tell him the truth about who she really was and how she had come to be handling the drilling on the Golden Slipper. She'd hoped to wait until they'd struck oil. But what if they didn't, she wondered uneasily. What if the worst happened and their discovery well turned up dry?

Josie pushed the nagging uncertainty away. She couldn't allow herself to think like that, she told herself sternly. That was her mother and father talking, not her. She knew how talented she was. She had proven it over and over again with her secret analysis and predictions on other discovery wells her father had dug.

"You're awfully quiet," Wade said, his hands softly stroking her hair. "Any particular reason why?"

One, Josie thought. And it was an important one. Her heart brimming with love and tenderness, she snuggled closer. She loved the warmth and solidity of his chest and the gentle way he held her in his arms. "I don't want there to be anything between us," she admitted softly. Especially now, when she felt so close to him. And yet there was, and it was a problem of her own making.

"That's why we're naked between the sheets," Wade teased.

Josie shifted her weight and rolled gracefully onto her side. She bent her elbow and propped her head up on her hand. Needing to reassure herself by touching him, she stroked a hand across his chest. "I mean I don't want us to have any secrets from each other," she said seriously. And soon, hopefully, they wouldn't.

He studied her, his mood abruptly turning as solemn as hers as he rubbed a hand up and down her spine. "I don't, either."

An awkward silence fell between them. A new wave of guilt sifted through Josie. Her cheeks turned pink. As he continued to study her, she felt as if she were up to her neck in quicksand. After a moment Wade's glance gentled and turned more pensive and self-effacing, too. "Look, I know establishing emotional intimacy with someone isn't my strong point." He swallowed, his eyes reflecting the depth of his regrets. He turned on his back, looked up at the ceiling and laid his forearm across his eyes. "Hell, to be honest—" his voice caught emotionally "—my difficulty in doing so is my biggest shortcoming."

Guilt flooded her as Josie realized Wade thought this was his fault! When it was so clearly hers! "You don't have to apologize," she said hastily, putting up a silencing hand to stop him from going any further.

Catching her hand, he kissed the back of it. Ignoring the easy out she gave him, he murmured gently, "But I'm willing to learn." He clamped an arm about her waist and drew her closer. "So what do you want to know?" he asked, as Josie draped one of her smooth sexy legs between his hair-roughened ones. "Just ask me and I'll tell you," he promised.

The phone rang before she could answer. Saved by the bell, Josie thought, aware she was relieved. Maybe they both were....

Her conscience still pricking mightily, demanding to be assuaged, Josie forced a smile and reached for the phone. "Might be Gus 'bout the drill-stem test." She was praying for a good result. One that would allow her to tell Wade the entire truth, so she could put this whole miserable ruse behind them.

But it wasn't Gus, Josie realized as she listened. And the instant reprieve she had hoped for wasn't to be. "Just a moment, please." Josie handed the phone to Wade. "It's for you."

Chapter 10

"Thanks, but no thanks," Wade said. "No. I'm aware of his father's reputation in commercial real estate. But it's his father's reputation, not his." Wade paused. "He may very well have his father's talent for putting together deals, but I'm not interested in having an inexperienced realtor put together a deal of that magnitude—I don't care what his vision—it's just too much money to risk. Yeah. Thanks." He hung up.

"Problem?" Josie asked, aware cold chills of uneasiness were coursing up and down her spine.

Wade lay back against the pillows, an exasperated expression on his face. "Some green kid wants me to go in on a new skyscraper in Houston. I've been avoiding his calls, so he had a mutual friend call me and ask me to reconsider, but there's no way."

Josie slipped from the bed and began to dress. "Did you hear his pitch?"

"No." With a disgruntled sigh, Wade got up, too.

"Why not?" Josie slipped her T-shirt over her head and tugged on her jeans. She zipped and buttoned them in short order. "It seems unfair to just turn him down cold."

Wade shrugged as he tugged on tight-fitting black briefs and then his jeans. "Maybe it is unfair but it's also good business sense." He slipped his shirt over his broad shoulders.

"I don't see it," Josie disagreed as she ran a brush through her hair. Gathering the silky length of it in one hand, she secured it to the back of her head with an elastic band. In fact, his attitude seemed downright unfair to her.

Wade strode toward her lazily, buttoning his shirt as he went. Still watching her as though he wanted nothing more than to make love to her again and again and again, he sat down and reluctantly tugged on his boots. "Houston and Dallas are filled with millionaire businessmen who made their fortunes in gas, oil and real estate. A lot of their kids think they'll follow in their parents' footsteps and join the family business. Unfortunately, because of their wealthy, pampered upbringing, 99 percent of them don't have the raw ambition and drive that their parents possessed, never mind an understanding of the kind of dedication required to be a success in today's difficult business climate. They think they can skate on their family's reputation and show up when they please. It doesn't work that way, but try explaining that to someone who doesn't even know he or she is a dilettante." Wade scowled and shook his head.

Josie dipped her finger into a pot of clear lip gloss and smoothed it over her lips. She pressed her lips together. "I think you're being unfair not to give the kid a chance."

"Maybe." Wade grinned unrepentantly. He rolled lazily to his feet and strode toward her. "But let him prove himself on someone else's buck, on someone else's time. I didn't get where I am today by making risky investments that ultimately don't pan out." He hooked an arm about her waist and drew her intimately close, so they were touching in one long electrified line. "Now, where were we?"

Getting ready to make the biggest mistake of my life, Josie thought, *and tell you everything before I'd proved myself as a wildcatter instead of after.*

Knowing she couldn't bear to make love with him again, with this secret still between them, Josie looked at her watch. "The drill-stem test results should be about ready." Hopefully they'd be good news.

Wade regarded her affectionately. "Want to head over there?"

Josie nodded and let out a wavering breath. "ASAP."

"Saltwater," Gus pronounced as they all gathered around to see what they had.

Josie studied the steady flow coming out of the test tool. It was all she could do not to swear. She had been certain—as had the rest of the guys—that they were on the edge of a major oil field. Not anywhere near as big as the one her father was drilling in South America, but a field that would produce hundreds of thousands of dollars worth of oil nonetheless. "Not even a hint of oil or gas," she said, feeling as disappointed as Dieter, Ernie, Gus and Wade.

"Well, what do you want to do?" Gus said as he turned the flow to a tank battery where it would be held for further analysis. "Drill deeper? Or call it a dry hole, cap it and sink another well somewhere else?"

Everyone looked at Josie. She was the one with the instincts. And instincts were telling her to keep going. "I say go deeper," she said determinedly. "See what we've got in another five hundred feet or so." Not surprisingly, Gus, Dieter and Ernie were in agreement with her, but there was someone else who should be consulted, too. Josie looked at Wade. "What do you think?"

He regarded her with complete confidence he would not have had, she knew, had he only known she was a former deb and heiress in her own right.

"Let's keep going," he said quietly, letting her know with a glance that he accepted what she recommended, and trusted her to make the right decision. Which, of course, under the circumstances, only made Josie feel more guilty. Nevertheless, Josie breathed a sigh of relief. She still had time—and the opportunity—to strike oil and make everything right.

"Okay, boys, let's shut her down and pull the test tool," Gus said.

Josie looked at the crew. They looked as tired and exhausted as she felt. Aware they had been working round the clock for days now, putting their blood, sweat and tears into the digging of this discovery well, just as she had, and that it would be several more hours before they would have the drill-stem test tool removed from the well and could resume drilling, she stuck her hands in the pockets of her jeans and said as cheerfully as possible, "Anyone up for sandwiches and coffee?"

"That depends." Gus grinned for the first time since they'd caught sight of the saltwater flowing out of the pipe. He peered at Josie. "You doing the cooking?"

Josie gave Gus a quelling look as the men started chuckling. "Don't look a gift horse in the mouth," she scolded, already climbing down from the derrick floor.

"Not to worry, guys," Wade winked, heading down the metal stairs after her. "I'll make the coffee."

Guffaws abounded.

Josie and Wade climbed in his Expedition and drove the short distance to her trailer. As they got out and headed for the front door, she—who was unable to mask her never-ending embarrassment over her lack of culinary expertise—said, "Everyone really hates my coffee, don't they?"

He hesitated, but in the end couldn't—wouldn't-lie to her. "It's probably not the best any of us have ever tasted, but it's probably not the worst, either," he said gently.

"Well, that's comforting," Josie said dryly.

"So I'll make the coffee." He shrugged his broad shoulders, letting her know with that simple gesture he wasn't looking so much for a housekeeper as a lover-companion-confidante. "So what?"

Josie clamped her lips together stubbornly. "So I don't like not being able to do something. That's what." Josie paused, aware she was about to take a monumental step here, and ask someone to help her change. And perhaps become a tad more domestic in the process. "Would you mind walking me through it and showing me what I'm doing wrong? 'Cause even though I'm loath to admit it, my coffee is lousy and yours is pretty good. Actually—" Josie blushed self-consciously "—it's excellent."

Wade grinned. He chucked her playfully beneath the chin. "Thanks."

"You're welcome." Josie tilted her face up to his. "So you'll help me out here?"

"That depends." Wade narrowed his eyes at her. He folded his arms in front of him. "You're really asking me to help you?"

"Yeah." Josie reflected briefly on all the time she'd spent resisting other people's efforts to help her change. Back then it had seemed somehow noble to hang on to every idiosyncratic inch of her personality, but now—especially when it came to something like this—it just seemed foolish. "I guess I am," Josie told Wade slowly. "But only—" she tapped his chest and inhaled the sexy, masculine fragrance that was him "—on the condition you don't make fun of me."

"I won't make fun of you," Wade promised huskily. He gathered her in his arms, using the flat of his hand to fit them together like matching pieces of a puzzle. Josie's breath caught in her throat. Wade smiled at her reaction to him, lowered his head ever so deliberately, and delivered a slow, languid kiss.

They were trembling as they drew apart. Much more of this, Josie knew, and they wouldn't get any coffee or sandwiches made. They had to stay on task here, she schooled herself sternly. At least for a little while. "Okay, where do we begin?" Josie asked, a little breathlessly. Her hands trembled as she reached over the dirty dishes stacked in the sink and rinsed out the coffee decanter, lid and plastic filter as best she could.

Wade put the stopper in the drain, turned the water temperature to hot and squirted dishwashing liquid under the stream. As silky bubbles filled the sink, he said, "We begin with a scrupulously clean coffeepot."

"Makes sense I guess," Josie murmured.

Wade helped her wash and rinse the components, and while they were at it, her breakfast dishes from that morning. When they were dry, they set them on the counter. He looked around at the jumble of cereal boxes, old newspapers and fruit rinds littering the counter. "Where's your coffee?"

"In the bag there—yeah, that's right, the open one—on the counter." Josie studied Wade's ruggedly handsome face. And knew it was one she would dream about forever.

Josie paused and bit her lip. "Why are you frowning?"

Wade gave her an indulgent look. He reached past her and snagged the coffee. "Because coffee should always be kept in a tightly sealed container," he explained softly.

"Oh." Maybe that was why her coffee never had a delicious aroma when it brewed, once it had been open awhile, Josie thought.

"But this'll do," Wade continued cheerfully. He rubbed his palms together. "Now, where are your filters?"

Uh-oh, Josie thought. She made a face. "I ran out earlier in the week—since then I've just been using paper towel to stop up the hole in the bottom of the plastic filter to sort of keep the grounds from dripping through."

He lifted a brow and regarded her with a curious look. "Does it work?"

"Uh…not really, no," Josie was forced to admit.

Wade did not look surprised about that. He muttered something she figured she probably was better off not understanding. "No good, huh?"

"Definitely not good, but it'll have to do." He lined the filter then asked, "Where's your coffee measure?"

Josie—who'd been momentarily distracted—drew her eyes from the sexy shape of his legs and hips and the glovelike fit of his jeans, front and back. "I, uh, I don't have one." If she was going to get anything at all out of this lesson, she was really going to have to stay on task, Josie thought.

"Got a tablespoon?" Wade asked, giving her a peculiar look. As Josie continued to look at him blankly, he added, "A real one."

Josie shook her head. Looking at Wade's lips was no good, either. She blinked. "Uh, no." She had to stop thinking about how much she liked his kisses. And caresses.

"Okay." Wade did his best with a regular tablespoon, adding one tablespoon per cup of ice-cold water. He snapped in the filter, then put the clear glass coffee decanter on the warmer.

Then he switched it on.

Seconds later, the coffee began to brew.

Josie got out the bread. Holding open the door to the fridge with her hip, she also handed out deli-sliced turkey, Swiss cheese and ham. "I didn't realize you had to be so precise." She grabbed some green olives, too, and added those to the sandwich makings on the counter.

Wade reached past her for mayo, mustard, pickles, lettuce and tomatoes.

"With certain things-like the amount of butter or sour cream you put on a baked potato—it doesn't matter," Wade replied. Tearing open the head of lettuce, he began to rinse the leaves. "But when it comes to other stuff—like making coffee or baking a cake—it really does."

Josie began laying out slices of bread, two at a time, across the counter.

"How do you know so much about cooking?" She'd always thought it was a feminine, domestic chore. Wade made it look anything but. In fact, he was so competent in this domain, even in someone else's kitchen, he made her a little envious.

"My mother insisted we all know how to cook a few things, whether we liked it or not. And the knowledge came in handy for all of us at one time or another. What about your parents?"

Josie added a slice of cheese to every sandwich, then additionally layered them with turkey and ham. Josie pressed her lips together regretfully. "My mother doesn't cook, never has, never will. If she needs coffee, and there's no one else around to make it for her, she goes out and buys some. Ditto for everything else, as she has no interest in anything at all domestic or house-frau-ish."

Wade laid the lettuce on paper towels to drain and sliced up the tomatoes, too. "What about your dad?"

"He cooks like I do—" Josie added mustard and mayo to the sandwiches "—haphazardly at best." Josie grinned. "Or maybe I should say I cook like he does, since he's the one who taught me what little I do know when we were out on various drilling sites. The trailer kitchens were never well equipped. Cookbooks or actual recipes were scoffed at. I was just expected to make do in a very unobtrusive way."

Wade layered slices of lettuce and tomato on each sandwich. "How old were you when all this was going on?" he asked lazily.

"Six when I started making peanut butter and jam sandwiches for the guys." Josie added tops to all the sandwiches they'd built. She looked over at Wade and smiled as he began cutting the sandwiches. "Eight or nine when I started making coffee. To tell the truth, I never graduated much beyond that because my results were always so lousy." Josie got out bags and began wrapping the sandwiches for the guys. "But I had other talents—like my ability to read geographical surveys and spot a good place to drop a well—that evened things out. So the guys respected me for that." Josie smiled, recalling how good that had felt then and still did.

Wade shook his head at her. "You must have been something, even then," he drawled admiringly.

Josie smiled and rolled her eyes. "I wasn't your average city girl, that's for sure."

Wade paused. "Was it hard—going back and forth between your mom and your dad?"

Josie sobered. "Yeah. It was." She stopped and shook her head, as if that would dispel some of the less happy memories. "It was such a delicate balancing act. I was always worried they'd stop loving me the way they stopped loving each other. Eventually, of course, I realized that wasn't true—that they would each love me in their own way no matter what—even if they couldn't get along with each other. But it was tough, always feeling as if I had to live up their considerable expectations, instead of being free just to be me."

Wade studied her. "Do you still feel pressured?" he asked softly, compassionately. Noting the coffee had stopped brewing, he went about filling an extralarge stainless steel thermos.

Josie grinned as she added paper cups, individual packets of sugar and powdered creamer to the stack of things they planned to take. "You mean by guys who expect me to know how to cook—or at least go out of my way to learn—and be a perfect lady?" she asked dryly.

"Touché." Wade lifted his hands in mea culpa fashion. His eyes gentled. "I'm sorry I tried to get you to change." He gathered her in his arms and stroked her hair. "I like you just the way you are," he said softly.

Josie's heart swelled. "I like you, too," she whispered back.

In fact, if the truth were known, she had fallen in love with him. And one day soon, the time would come to tell him that.

"You said you had something you wanted to talk

about or ask me," Wade said as they packed up the sandwiches and the coffee and carried both back out to his Expedition.

And she still did, Josie thought. But now was not the time, knowing how he felt about dilettantes and heirs who took advantage of their parents' business reputations. Like it or not she was going to have to prove herself first, then level with him and tell him everything.

With effort, Josie shook off her guilt and the worry and intolerable frustration of having to wait that went right along with it. "It wasn't important," she said with a smile. Not compared to all the love and tenderness they had just shared.

"Sure?" Wade studied her intently.

Josie nodded. She'd tell him later, she decided. When the time was right. When he would have reason to forgive her. And not a second before.

Together they drove over to the site. They opened up the back of Wade's Expedition and laid out the food like a tailgate picnic. Figuring it would be better to eat down there, away from the vibration and the noise of the machinery, they set off to get the guys.

"How's it going?" Josie asked as she and Wade climbed the derrick steps to join them.

Gus grinned and gave her a thumbs-up sign. "We've almost got the test tool out."

Without warning, there was a strange rumbling sound and a faint, slightly irregular vibration. It seemed to be coming from the center of the earth up. All five of them stopped dead in their tracks. None of them moving, none of them daring to so much as breathe as they exchanged tense, wary looks.

"Is that what I think it is?" Wade asked incredulously.

A second later he had his answer as black oil surged up out of the hole, a little bubble at first, then in a growing, pulsing stream that showered the floor of the derrick and the tops of their heads and the ground around them, and left no doubt at all what it was they had hit.

"Oil!" Josie shouted with all-out joy and disbelief, the guys whooping and hollering all around her as she rushed forward to hit the switch that would shut it down. "We struck oil!"

Wade grabbed her around the middle and lifted her clear off her feet. He brought her against him and gave her a Texas-size kiss. "We did it!" he shouted.

Josie grinned and hugged him back, hard. She kissed him, too. Exuberantly at first, then with growing tenderness. She drew back. Beaming, she looked up at him and hugged him again, hard. "We sure did, cowboy. We sure did."

Josie's next thirty-six hours were filled with work, and Wade was with her every step of the way, documenting the discovery, temporarily capping the well, arranging for the oil to be sold. Figuring out where and when the next well—on the opposite edge of the oil field—should be dug. Suddenly it was Friday noon. And the party for Wade's parents was in just five hours.

Wade appeared in Josie's office. Noting no one else was around—not that it would have mattered, as the rest of the guys had long since figured out what was going on between them—Wade crossed the distance between them in three long strides. Before she could do more than rake in one quick breath, he wrapped his arms around her, pressed his lips to hers, firmly, possessively. She kissed him back, just as hungrily, knowing in a moment she would have to get back to the business at hand, but wanting—for this moment, anyway—only to feel and luxuriate in the fast-growing affection and tenderness they'd found. Eventually, reluctantly, he let the kiss come to a halt. Still holding her close, he looked down at her.

She studied him, too—his eyes so soft and compelling against the thick fringe of ash brown lashes, his windswept untidy hair, sunburned cheeks and nose, the stubborn set of his jaw, the sensual shape of his lips. It was so easy to see why she had fallen head over heels in love with him. Easier still to realize why she could no longer envision her life without him. He'd brought her joy. A willingness to bend. The belief that two people really did belong together sometimes. That sometimes they needed to give as well as receive.

He murmured, "I asked Gus, Ernie and Dieter all to come to the party tonight."

She moved closer, delighting in the feeling of having her body mold against his. She smiled up at him. "That was nice of you."

His palms stroked up and down her back. "I want 'em to come. I figure they've all earned a night out."

Josie looked up at his clean-shaven jaw. It felt so right, being with him here like this. Sharing their work, sharing their lives. "Do they know it's black tie?"

Wade nodded. "I'm having some tuxedos sent out for them. Meanwhile, I've got to go into town to the community center to see how things are progressing there.

Want to ride along?" He waggled his eyebrows at her comically. "To tell you the truth, I could use the help." Tilting his head, he studied her.

Josie hugged him briefly, then tucked her hand in his. She'd be happy to go anywhere with him. "Sure, I'll go." In fact, she'd be delighted.

At the community center, it was pure bedlam. The caterers were at odds with the florist, who were at odds with the musicians, who were trying to set up to rehearse. Wade took one look at all the activity and didn't know where to begin. Josie took one look and grinned. "Definitely a work in progress," she drawled, already rolling up her sleeves.

Wade looked tense, worried and completely out of his element. "Can you help?"

"Oh, yeah." Josie stood on a chair, put two fingers between her teeth and let out a whistle that would stop New York City traffic. As it had in the past, it worked like a charm. Every eye turned her way as all activity stopped. "I want the representative in charge of every company here." Josie pointed to the table in front of her. "Meanwhile everyone else just sit tight."

Ten minutes later she had listened to everyone's grievances, sorted out the conflicts, given the orders and had Wade working on hanging the congratulatory banner. It took two more hours, but when they were finished they had transformed the rec center into the themed Time Capsule that Josie had helped Wade to envision. A slide show of photos, recapping Lilah's and John's lives as community healers was all set to go. At the far end of the gaily decorated room, up on the stage, was the architectural model of the new hospital wing being donated in Lilah's and John's names. Wade had covered it with a deep blue velvet blanket to ensure secrecy.

"Think they'll be surprised?" he asked Josie.

As surprised as I was to find myself falling in love with you, Josie thought. She nodded, feeling happier and more content than she ever had in her life. "I talked to Meg a few minutes ago. She said the staff was taking turns keeping them busy over at the hospital—your parents haven't a clue about tonight—they still think they're attending the society wedding of one of Mayor Moore's cousins, whom they delivered years ago. Your dad is still arguing against wearing a tuxedo."

"But my mother—"

"—is insisting he do it, anyway," Josie supplied.

Wade breathed a sigh of relief. "Good."

Josie grinned. "Speaking of getting all gussied up." Josie looked down at her own shirt, jeans and boots. "Any chance I could catch a ride with you back to the ranch?"

He tugged the end of her ponytail affectionately. "There's every chance."

They rode back in silence, feeling exhausted and excited. Once again Josie wanted to tell Wade who she was and how she had come to take the job drilling for oil on his ranch, but once again she knew the timing was all off. Her dishonesty was likely to upset him. She didn't want him upset on the night his parents were being honored. The information would keep until tomorrow, but then she would definitely have to tell him. And then get down on her hands and knees and beg his forgiveness and swear never ever to do anything remotely like it ever again.

Wade stopped his truck in front of her trailer. He turned toward her and draped his arm along the back of the seat. "I'll be back in an hour. Will that give you enough time?"

Josie nodded, knowing she had her work cut out for her if she was going to transform herself from tomboy into the Texas princess of Wade's dreams. But it was a challenge she was up to. "More than enough."

"Problem?" Wade asked as the shoeless Josie let him in the door.

Flushing hotly, for she couldn't recall when she had been so embarrassed, Josie covered one stocking-clad foot with the other and gestured at the collection of tennis shoes, galoshes and boots in front of her. "I forgot I didn't bring any dress shoes from home when I moved out here." She'd left her entire collection of designer pumps and evening sandals at her home in Dallas. "And we also forgot to pick up the boots you were having made for me—" Which left her, Josie noted, in the incredibly fragile evening dress of silk-chiffon.

"You forgot," Wade interrupted, his hot, appreciative glance taking in the uppermost swell of her breasts, spilling out of her lavender-mauve dress. "I didn't. I had them sent out with the tuxedos for the guys."

Still grinning, he presented her with a ribbon-wrapped box, then got down on one knee in front of her, like some knight errant, protecting his queen. He looked sexy and handsome as all get-out in his black tuxedo and pleated white shirt. The bracing fragrance of his sandalwood and leather cologne clung to his skin, immersing Josie in memories of their lovemaking and the kisses they had shared. And would share again. "Allow me," he said softly in a low, husky voice that only made her want him all the more.

Her heart pounding, Josie sat down on the edge of the sofa. Everything she had ever wanted or needed was right here, with the two of them.

To her surprise, it wasn't so much having her first real success in the oil business, as finding the love of her life. And knowing he was every bit as besotted with her as she was with him.

Shooting him an amused look—it was a revelation to discover she rather liked being treated as the Cinderella he had envisioned and wanted her to be from the very first—Josie hiked up the long skirt of her evening dress. Looking as if he were enjoying the process immensely, Wade took the kicky satin evening boots, dyed the same shade as her dress, and fit them on her feet. Grinning all the more, he began the slow, sexy work of lacing them up. Luxuriating in the feel of his warm, capable hands cupping her calves and closing around her ankles, she let out her breath in a long sigh.

Finished, he helped her to her feet and took her into his arms. Gave her a slow, measured look. "You know," he drawled huskily as he ran a hand lovingly down her face, "if we didn't have to be there before my parents to orchestrate the surprise, I'd say to heck with getting there early or even on time, and I'd carry you into that bedroom and make hot, wild love to you all evening long." He ran his fingertip along her collarbone and felt her pulse jump. His lips were warm and firm on hers. "You know that, don't you?"

"I'm beginning to," Josie admitted breathlessly. Whatever happened tomorrow or the next day or the day after that, she would never forget what they had shared.

He kissed her again. And then again. Until both were trembling. Aching. He pulled back reluctantly, the need in his eyes matching hers. "We'd better go," he told her huskily, "or we won't get there at all."

Chapter 11

"So there really were no lessons on how to be a lady," Lilah said to Wade and Josie, once the surprise had been revealed and the party for Wade's folks was in full swing.

Josie looked at Wade, who, not surprisingly, had begun to look a tad sheepish. "Actually," she hedged, laughter in her low voice.

Heat climbing into his face, Wade laced an arm about Josie's waist. He admitted good-naturedly, "I did try to teach her a thing or two."

John surveyed Josie, the way a father surveys his son's prospective bride. Amusement in his eyes, he drawled, "Hate to tell you this, son, but it doesn't look to me like Josie needs any help in that regard."

Josie grinned and looked up at Wade. It pleased her to have John and Lilah's approval. It seemed to please

Wade, too. Tucking her hand in Wade's, she turned back to his folks. "I couldn't resist pulling his leg a little when he 'decided' I was too much of a tomboy for my own good." She shrugged. "So I let him teach me how to dance."

Wade brought Josie closer. "But it was Josie who ended up teaching me a thing or two."

Lilah smiled. "Well, I couldn't be happier for the two of you. It's about time Wade stopped trying to make over all his dates and accepted the woman in his life for who and what she is, without wishing she were otherwise."

The only problem, Josie thought uncomfortably, was that Wade didn't know yet who and what she really was, and she wasn't sure how he would react when he did find out. But she wouldn't think about that now, she decided firmly. Tonight was the fulfillment of all the Cinderella dreams she'd had when she was a kid. She was here with her Prince Charming, and she was going to enjoy herself. Midnight—the end of the party and the return to reality—would come soon enough.

"Things must be going pretty well with Wade McCabe," Meg Lockhart said to Josie later, at the punch bowl.

Josie picked up two glasses of champagne punch and drank deeply of one of them. "What makes you say that?"

Meg smiled, the nurturing side of her in full evidence. "You're glowing with happiness," she murmured approvingly.

Josie set her glass down on the table and topped it up once again. On the other side of the rec center, she could see Wade exactly where she'd left him—deep in conversation with his three brothers. He looked handsome and debonair in his sexy black tux. Just looking at him, she felt her heart do a funny little hop. "It's that evident," she murmured, thinking how ardently he had kissed her earlier and how he had promised to do so again as soon as the party had ended.

"Oh, yes." Meg nodded. She swept a hand down the side of her pastel yellow evening gown. "When I walked in and saw you and Wade standing together—" Meg shook her head in awe "—I've got to tell you. I've known him for years and I've never seen him look quite so dazzled by any woman," she finished softly.

Josie knew she couldn't take complete credit for that, even though she had wanted to look her best for Wade that evening and done her hair and makeup with care. "It's the gown Mother sent."

Meg shook her head, disagreeing. "It's you." She smiled warmly. "But as long as we're speaking of Bitsy." Meg paused, took a sip of her own punch, then leaned close and whispered confidentially, "Was your mother able to track you down before the party?"

Josie shook her head. She felt a tad guilty about that. "She called a few times the past couple of days and left messages on my machine, asking me to call her back, but I haven't had time." Josie frowned. Even as she had done that, she knew it was a mistake. No one ignored Bitsy for long.

Meg scanned the crowd casually, then turned back to Josie. She took another sip of punch. "But you do know she's back in Laramie again, right?"

"What?" Josie was so startled she almost dropped her punch.

"Oh, yeah. She got in late this afternoon. She stopped by the hospital to see if I could give her the lowdown on what had been going on with you."

"You didn't tell her we'd struck oil out there, did you?" Josie asked, horrified, knowing *that* more than anything would have sent her mother straight for Josie.

"Yes. I did. But I also told her you were giving a party for a friend this evening and probably wouldn't be back at the site till sometime tomorrow morning."

Thank heaven for small miracles. "What did she say to that?"

Meg smiled. "She was happy you were helping someone throw a party."

Which wasn't surprising, Josie thought, given the premium her mother put on entertaining and social-izing in general. "Well, at least I have a little time to prepare for our confrontation." Which would probably happen first thing tomorrow morning, Josie thought with a sigh.

"You think she's going to be that upset?"

Josie rolled her eyes. "When I tell her—now that I've had success in the oil business—that I have no intention of working at the Corbett Foundation ever again? You bet she'll be upset." She would probably lecture Josie nonstop for several hours on the error of her ways.

Meg smiled at Josie sympathetically. "But she'll be happy you found oil and have fallen in love with an up and comer like Wade McCabe."

Josie grinned, unable to hide her happiness about that. "Who said I was in love?" she chided, amused.

Meg laughed softly. "You didn't have to say it," she teased. "It's written all over your face."

The question was, Josie wondered, did Wade feel the same way. He hadn't come out and said the words yet. But he sure was acting as if he was. And that fact alone made her heart sing.

Meg's eyes clouded. "Uh-oh."

"What?" Josie said, alarmed by the look of concern on her friend's face.

Meg stepped protectively in front of Josie, blocking her from view. "Don't look now, but your mother's here," she said in a low concerned tone. Meg shook her head. "And you are never going to guess who she's got with her."

"So what do you think about the sudden upswing in the price of technology stocks the last couple of days?" Travis asked Wade as the four McCabe brothers gathered around the architectural model of the new hospital wing that was going to be built in honor of their parents. "Is it worth moving some of the money I've got in bonds over to those stocks?" Travis continued curiously. "Or should I keep my money where it is?"

Wade blinked. He forced himself to concentrate on his cattle-ranching brother. "Technology stocks went up?"

Travis's brows rose in surprise. He looked at Wade in concern. "There was a 10 percent jump across the board in the last three days." He paused, clearly stunned, as everyone in the McCabe family knew how often Wade checked his stock prices. It was practically a religion with him. Travis continued to study his younger brother. "You didn't hear about it?" he asked, stunned.

Wade shook his head, surprised at how unexcited he was by the news he had just upped his net worth another hundred thousand or so. "I haven't had time to even get on the computer or watch the news the last couple of days." What was more telling still was the fact he didn't mind not knowing what had been going on with the market.

Maybe he had changed.

Travis, Jackson and Shane exchanged looks. "You've got it bad, Brother," Shane drawled as all eyes turned from the architectural model of the new hospital wing to Wade.

Wade grinned. He knew he was in love with Josie. Before the night was out, she'd know it, too.

"Better watch out," Travis continued, teasing, "or before you know it you'll be getting married, too."

Wade knew that was true. In fact, given his druthers he'd run away with Josie tonight to say their I do's. And that was amazing, too. But true.

Lilah joined her sons. She was dressed in a beaded pale pink gown. There was warm color in her cheeks and happiness in her eyes. "You boys all look so handsome tonight." She beamed at all of them with motherly pride, then turned to Wade and shook her head slowly in admiration. "I don't know how you pulled this off—"

Wade smiled, glad he finally had the means to do what they all had wanted to do for his parents and the entire Laramie community for years.

"The party is wonderful!" Lilah continued, admiring the stage band playing swing and jazz and country-western tunes.

"Josie gets the credit for that." Without her, Wade didn't know what he would have done. It certainly wouldn't have been much of a party from a flowers, food and entertainment standpoint, anyway.

Lilah's smile softened and her eyes sparkled romantically. "She looks beautiful tonight, doesn't she?"

Yes, Wade thought, she did. And it was more than the sexy lavender-mauve gown she wore or the feminine way she'd done up her hair—in fancy curls pinned to the back of her head—and makeup. She was beautiful from the inside out tonight, glowing with an inner happiness and contentment only loving could bring. His only complaint was she'd been so busy playing hostess she'd hardly been at his side. But the evening was still young. They had plenty of time to get in some dancing and maybe sneak in a few kisses somewhere, too, before they headed back to his place for a night of wild and wonderful loving.

Lilah looked around and frowned. "Where is she, by the way?"

Wade scanned the room and did not find her, either. But maybe that wasn't surprising. He consulted his watch. "She's probably back in the kitchen, talking to the caterers. They're going to start serving dinner in a few minutes." He paused, aware none of the details of entertaining seemed to come as naturally to him as they did to Josie. "I better go see if she needs any help."

"Good idea." Lilah smiled. "Give her a kiss for me when you find her."

"Will do," Wade promised easily. His pulse picking

up in anticipation of the soft surrender of her lips beneath his, he threaded his way through the throngs of people his parents had helped over the years, stopping to talk to Gus, who was visiting with a retired toolmaker. Then met Ernie and Dieter midway. They were well into the appetizers and champagne. "You guys doing okay?" Wade asked, figuring he should do his bit as host, too.

"We're having a great time," Ernie said as he surveyed the vast array of appetizers that had been put out for the guests.

"Yeah. Never figured we'd be getting to go to something like this when Josie hired us," Dieter agreed, helping himself to some more champagne. "But then it's been a month of surprises, hasn't it, Ernie?"

Ernie nodded.

Wade blinked as the meaning of their words sunk in. "Big Jim didn't hire you?" Wade asked, sure he had misunderstood, but wanting it cleared up, anyway.

Ernie shrugged and popped a miniature meatball into his mouth. "Never met him."

A warning chill slid down Wade's spine. He had never known anyone to work on Big Jim's crew without interviewing with Big Jim personally first.

Ernie speared several pieces of coconut shrimp and placed them on a small crystal appetizer plate. "We almost weren't sure we wanted to hire on with Wyatt Drilling when we found out we'd be working for a woman if we took the job." Ernie added cucumber spears and a dollop of ranch dip to his plate, too. "But Josie convinced us she knew what she was doing. And why wouldn't she—considering the fact she'd been learning the business from her daddy almost since the day she was born."

"So it's worked out for you professionally?" Wade asked casually. Even if he himself had taken the brunt of the risk financially, he thought angrily.

Ernie nodded. "Oh, yeah. Josie's taught us a lot about the part gut instinct plays in this business."

Dieter agreed. "And so has Gus."

Too bad she hadn't shared any of the truth with him, Wade thought.

Ernie elbowed Dieter, who in turn elbowed Wade. "Hey, there she comes now."

"She sure does look pretty tonight," Dieter drawled as Josie threaded her way, almost surreptitiously, through the crowd of five hundred plus elegantly clad guests.

Ernie nodded. "Like Cinderella at the ball."

Seconds later Josie joined them. Not surprisingly, Wade noted, she looked flushed and uneasy as well as damn beautiful. And somehow worried to boot. The question was, why hadn't he noticed earlier? Had he been that besotted? Or had something happened in the few minutes they'd been apart to change everything? Besides him finding out the truth. Damn it, how could she have kept such a secret from him? He wondered, incensed. And how many more were there?

Josie scanned the crowd behind them, then looked from Dieter and Ernie to Wade. Obviously she had picked up on the tension in him, Wade thought. Which meant she was a lot more observant about what was going on with him than he had been about what was really happening with her. "What's going on?" she asked.

Wade forced a smile. "Ernie and Dieter were just telling me how glad they are that you—and not Big Jim—hired them."

As Wade's coolly uttered words sank in, Josie felt all the blood drain from her face. So much for taking risks, she thought miserably. Catching a fleeting glimpse of her mother threading her way through the crowd, she grabbed Wade's wrist and tugged him behind a large potted plant. "I can explain," she said hurriedly. She only hoped he would give her a chance.

Wade stood, legs braced apart, arms folded in front of him. "I think I already know." He regarded her with grim confidence.

Josie paused, her heart racing in a painful, jerky rhythm. She stared at him in confusion. "You do?" How was that possible?

"In your eagerness to prove yourself worthy of a drilling supervisor position at Wyatt Drilling, you overstepped your bounds and took charge at the site."

Josie swallowed. That was part of it. "You're right," she said in a low voice, aware this was most definitely not the time or place, or the way she had ever wanted to get into this. She propped her hands on her waist, tilted her chin at him and hitched in a trembling breath. "I did."

A muscle ticked in his cheek. "And that's it—that's all you have to say?" he demanded roughly.

No, of course it wasn't, Josie thought, as she saw her

mother edging ever closer. But there was also no time to spare. She darted past Wade. "I've got to go."

He caught her by the arm and swung her around to face him. "What?"

Josie put up her hands to stave him off. There was still a chance for this to work out right. But it would take a peaceful setting and a great deal of privacy—two things they didn't have. "I don't have time to explain," Josie said hurriedly, wishing like heck she did even as she spoke. She stepped away from him. "But everything's all set," she told him, hanging on to her composure by a thread. "The dinner's about to be served, the orchestra is going to fill in with recordings when they are on break, and the bartenders have an unlimited supply of champagne, punch and various soft drinks, as well as a bevy of drivers on standby for anyone needing rides home." She dashed around the potted plant.

Wade dashed after her. "I want you with me tonight."

"And I want to be here." Tears pricked Josie's eyes. "You don't know how much. But—" Josie caught sight of her mother again. In a panic she ducked into the supply room, taking Wade with her. She shut the door behind her, being careful to make as little noise and attract as little attention as possible. "I just can't."

Wade narrowed his eyes at her. Without warning, he looked just about out of patience. "Why are you behaving so strangely all of a sudden?" he demanded.

Josie gulped, very much aware she was on the verge of losing everything. And would if she didn't handle things right. "I've got some important things to do."

His hands moved to her waist. He pulled her against

him and held her close. Beneath the confusion in his eyes was the love. "This evening is important, too."

Guilt flooded her anew. "I know but I just can't be here. Something's come up, and I've got to take care of it."

His lips tightened and the expression in his eyes grew colder. "What aren't you telling me?" he demanded, knowing by now it was something.

She took a calming breath but it didn't help. "I... it's...complicated."

"So?" He pushed an impatient hand through his hair. "I can understand complicated things."

"I don't have time." Josie held up her hands beseechingly. She knew under the circumstances she had no right to ask, but she was going to do it, anyway. "Would you please trust me to be able to make the right decision here?"

Sadness and uncertainty warred in his eyes. "Josie, damn it—"

"I'll talk to you later." Josie broke away from him and turned toward the door. Grasping the doorknob with a clammy hand, she opened it a sliver to peer out, then groaned as the person on the other side of it caught a glimpse of her—and her memorable dress—and pushed it open all the way.

"I knew she was hiding from us!" Bitsy Corbett fumed. Like the rest of the guests there, she was attired in an evening dress. The same could not be said for the giant of a man next to her who was clad in jeans, a plaid shirt and leather vest and a battered straw cowboy hat.

Josie groaned as she realized several of her nightmares were coming true simultaneously. "Mother, please. Not here and not now."

But it was too late. Wade had already done a double take at the larger-than-life figure standing beside Josie's mother. "Big Jim?"

Big Jim extended his beefy hand and engulfed Wade's palm in a hearty handshake. "Nice to see you, McCabe."

Wade blinked. "I thought you were in South America."

"I was," Big Jim admitted, "till Bitsy moved heaven and earth to get a message to me and let me know we had a crisis on our hands."

Josie looked at her parents. The two had never seemed a more incongruous couple than they did at that instant, Josie thought miserably.

Still looking very glad to see him, Jim quirked a brow at Wade. "I hear congratulations are in order— you struck oil at the Golden Slipper Ranch?"

Wade nodded happily. "Thanks to the help of Josie here, yeah. I have to admit I was inclined to just pull the plug on the whole operation when I found her in charge. But she talked me out of it, and of course now I'm glad she did."

As Josie listened to the exchange, she found herself getting redder and redder.

"I know that wasn't quite what we agreed upon when you left for South America," Josie told her father nervously.

"Isn't that the understatement of the year," Big Jim shot right back, giving her a very definitive look.

"But we can talk about it elsewhere," Josie amended hastily, doing her best to conceal her panic.

"You're darn right we're going to talk about it," Big Jim fumed as Josie stood there rubbing her temples. "If you'll excuse us, McCabe, Bitsy and I'd like a word with our daughter."

"Daughter!" Wade echoed furiously.

He looked at Josie, clearly stunned. "You introduced yourself to me as Josie Lynn Corbett!"

"It's Corbett Wyatt," Bitsy supplied with equal parts helpfulness and censure.

Hating the hurt and betrayal she saw in Wade's eyes, Josie nodded jerkily at her parents. Stage band music floated in from the large party room beyond, giving the scene an almost surreal aura. "Since they were getting divorced, they wanted me to have both of their last names," she explained numbly. She wished she had pockets to hide her trembling fingers in. Since she didn't, she clamped her hands together behind her. "They figured it'd be easier for kids at school and so on, and it was."

"Not to mention when she went to work at the Corbett Foundation," Bitsy said, all too glad to explain further.

Unfortunately, the last thing Wade needed—in Josie's estimation—was another surprise. Wade turned to glare at her sharply. "You're related to those Corbetts? The Dallas, Texas, Corbetts?" Wade asked Josie in dismay. "That's the foundation you worked for? The Corbett Foundation?"

"Don't tell me Josie didn't tell you she's an heiress, either!" Bitsy fumed.

"Mother, please!" Josie said miserably. She turned to Wade. "I was going to tell you all, just as soon as I could."

"Were you." Wade shook his head in silent censure of all that had happened.

"Just like you were going to tell me you were using funds from your trust fund to finance the continued drilling on the Golden Slipper Ranch?" Bitsy reminded unhappily.

Josie bit her lip. Her whole world was falling apart, and she had only to look at Wade to know how furious he was about everything that was being revealed here tonight. Finding her trembling knees would no longer support her, Josie sank down on a step stool. "I wish you hadn't said that," Josie muttered. It made her look like that much more of a dilettante in Wade's eyes.

Bitsy moved closer, the diamonds at her throat and in her ears glinting in the fluorescent light. "Honestly, Josie, did you really think that I wouldn't call your father to let him know that you had decided to move part of your money over to Wyatt Drilling accounts?"

At mention of that little bit of ingenuity, Big Jim exploded. "Damn it, Josie, we have money set aside for exploration at Wyatt Drilling!" he scolded. "Had you just asked—"

"And how could I have done that?" Josie retorted hotly. "You were out in the jungle at the time and incommunicado, remember?" Josie surged to her feet and pointed at Wade. "He was about to pull the plug on the whole operation when he found out a woman was in charge."

Wade folded his arms in front of him. "It didn't

seem like something you would have done," Wade told Big Jim.

"You're right," Big Jim agreed sagely. "I wouldn't have left Josie in charge of your drilling project or any other."

"Right. If left up to you, all I ever would have been able to do is file papers and answer telephones at Wyatt Drilling!" Josie exploded. "If it had been left up to you, I never would have been given a chance to prove myself!"

Big Jim frowned. "That's because you don't belong in the oil fields," he said gently.

Josie felt herself go white, then red. "That's not what you said when I was a kid!" She countered hotly.

Big Jim took off his straw hat and slapped it against his knee. "That's because I wanted to spend time with you! I wasn't asking you to take on wildcatting as a career."

"But a career in wildcatting is what I wanted!" Josie told her father passionately.

Big Jim's lips tightened. "The oil fields are no place for a woman." He turned to Bitsy for help. "Ask your mother."

"I don't have to ask my mother." Josie tossed her head indignantly. "I know you don't belong there, Mom. You never did. But I do belong there, and furthermore I proved it when I talked Gus into helping me, hired my own crew and struck oil with the very first discovery well I dug."

"How did that happen, by the way?" Wade asked curiously, his eyes turning even grimmer. "Because I sent over a contract and it was returned to me with a signature."

Josie flushed bright red. "I signed my own initials, JLW, which happen to be the same as Big Jim's," Josie admitted reluctantly. She held up both hands in a gesture of surrender. She had never been more miserable or ashamed of herself in her life. "And before any of you say anything else," she said huskily as tears pricked her eyes, "I know I never should have done it. I knew it almost the moment after I had express-mailed the contracts back to your office, Wade."

"Then why didn't you call it quits then?" Wade asked.

Josie flushed even more beneath his close scrutiny. "Because I didn't want Wyatt Drilling to lose out on a lucrative contract just because my father had taken a consulting job for a big oil company in South America," she replied quietly. "Because I saw it as a chance to take the kind of risks I've always been afraid to take. Because I knew I could do it, and I wanted everyone else to know it, too." She looked at Wade steadily. "You were never going to lose money on the deal, nor was Wyatt Drilling. I knew from the beginning I'd use my trust funds to repay both if the well came up dry."

"Which is why you kept digging when everyone else would have been tempted to quit," Wade theorized.

"No," Josie corrected in frustration, upset. "I kept digging because I knew the oil was there on the property, and I knew it was on that particular site." Josie swiveled around. She turned to Big Jim, needing him to understand why and what she had done, too. "All the studies aside, I can't explain how I know—I just do. Just like you know, Dad."

"You should have told me," Wade interrupted, drawing her attention to him once again.

"You should have told all of us," Bitsy and Big Jim agreed.

"But I didn't," Josie said sadly. She laced her hands together. "And I can't go back and change that now. All I can do is apologize for my duplicity and the fact I went over the line this one time in my life, and try to move forward with the career of my choosing. Which happens to be wildcatting. The question is," she paused for a heartbeat of silence as she read the mixture of angst and disappointment on their faces, "are any of you going to forgive me?"

Silence rebounded in the storeroom. Outside, they could hear the music and the sounds of the party. "Of course we can forgive you," Big Jim said gruffly. He enveloped Josie in a big bear hug.

Bitsy hugged Josie, too. "Though I'd feel better if you gave up this lunacy and came back to work for the foundation," Bitsy added, as the two women drew apart.

"Mother—" Josie gave her a look.

Only Wade had remained silent.

Noticing, Big Jim turned to Bitsy. "Maybe we should take this up with Josie tomorrow, now that we know she's okay," he told Bitsy gently.

Bitsy nodded.

"Feel free to join the others for dinner, dancing and champagne," Wade said smoothly.

"Thanks," Bitsy and Big Jim said together. "We will."

Josie's parents departed. The awkward silence between them deepened. His disappointment in her evident, Wade stared down at Josie grimly. "I'm sorry," she said.

"So am I. Not so much about what you've done, although that in itself is bad enough, but about everything you didn't feel you could tell me."

The lack of understanding in his eyes was as chilling to her as the thought of a life without him. In a panic she edged close enough to see the brooding glint in his eyes, the stubborn set to his jaw. "You're angry."

"Hell, yes." Wade compressed his lips into a thin white line. He braced his hands on his waist and glared down at her. "Can you blame me?"

Josie paused, took a careful breath. She had to make him see what he was doing before it was too late. "For your reluctance to even give me a chance to apologize for what I've done and make amends?" she said softly, looking him straight in the eye. "Yes, Wade, I can blame you for that." Just as she blamed herself for the bulk of this mess.

"Why didn't you tell me who you were?" Wade demanded furiously, aware—as was she—that Josie'd had plenty of opportunities to confide in him, and she hadn't.

Feeling as if the words had thorns, she said, very carefully, "I didn't know how you'd react. Especially since I knew—in other cases—you had refused to get involved with someone who had their job by virtue of nepotism. What was it you said—business and nepotism were a bad risk? And because you'd already been burned by Andrea, the caterer, and thus had suffered your fill of what you called dilettantes and debs." Josie swallowed. "I didn't want you to think I was the same thing, and I knew, at least on the surface, it certainly looked that way. And there was so much money involved here—it just seemed to make it even worse, especially from your point of view."

Great. Another person who thought he had a cash register for a heart, Wade thought bitterly. Which was ironic, because around her he'd been all heart. "The truth is," Wade conceded grimly, so full of pain and fury he didn't know whether to shake her or hug her, "you'd have been happier if you'd never had to tell me what you'd done. Wouldn't you?"

"Of course," Josie said, looking at him as if it were ridiculous of him to even ask. She had never wanted to feel the way she felt right now. She had never wanted to be in a position again where she'd have to constantly worry she'd make a misstep and feel his crushing disappointment in her. She'd never wanted to be in a position where she'd have to constantly worry that Wade would leave her, like her dad had left her mother, because she wasn't going to be the kind of wife or woman Wade wanted.

She didn't want him to leave because the fling was over and he was just looking for a way out. Any more than she wanted him to leave because he didn't want to be married to a wildcatter.

She wanted to be free to be who she was, to know she could make mistakes and still be loved. She wanted to know that forgiveness was an option, that she no longer had to prove herself every second of every day. But judging by the disillusioned look on his face, it didn't look as though that was going to happen, either, Josie realized sadly.

Wade backed her to the door and caged her with his arms. "Would you also be happier if we had never gone to bed together—never gotten involved?" he demanded, looking even more betrayed

Josie swallowed. "You make it sound cold-blooded," she murmured hotly. Like she'd had a choice in the dictates of her heart.

He cut her off with a scoff of contempt. "I'd say the deception part of it had to be cold-blooded."

Josie stiffened. She held her head high as she forced herself to admit, "I regretted not being able to talk to you, to tell you what was in my heart, more than you'll ever know." Her voice caught; she had to force herself to go on. "But I also knew it would be better—for you, for me, for my father and his company—to discuss all this after our business had been concluded in a positive manner."

Wade quirked a brow. "I see. You just didn't trust me to be capable of understanding or sympathizing with your predicament."

Josie drew a breath. She was darned if she was going to take the entire blame for this! "You don't seem to be understanding very well now," she said evenly, studying the ruggedly handsome lines of his face.

"Maybe because I just found out I slept with a woman I damn near fell in love with and asked to marry me—who didn't think I had enough heart in me to be there for her when and how she needed me to be there."

Josie was silent, realizing her buttons hadn't been

the only ones that had been pushed. He'd been hurt, too. Badly.

Tears gathered in her eyes. "You're right. I didn't trust you—or us—enough to level with you right away. But when I see you reacting the way you are now, I know I was right to worry how you'd take it." She curved her fingers around his biceps, hoping to get to him with touch in a way she wasn't able to with words. The rigidity of his arms, the fact he clearly did not want her touching him, made her drop her grip.

She swallowed hard around the gathering knot of emotion in her throat. "I don't want a relationship like my parents', Wade, any more than I want to make my parents' mistakes. They walked away from each other when they found out they weren't perfect, when they disappointed each other. They never gave their relationship a chance. They just decided to call it quits. I want someone who will give me a second chance when I need one." Josie tipped her head back. She paused and wet her lips, knowing she had never been more vulnerable in her life than she was at that instant. "Can you do that?" she whispered softly, emotionally. "Can you give me a second chance?"

Wade shook his head. He stepped back, away from the door, away from her. "No," he said softly, heavily, "I can't."

Chapter 12

"I've got just about everything ready to turn over to you, Dad," Josie told Big Jim as she greeted her parents from the doorway of her trailer and ushered them inside. She had been up all night, preparing to hand over the reins and get her dad—and whoever he selected to replace her—up to speed. Josie picked up a stack of folders from her desk. "Here's the chronology of the drilling, every single aspect of it, recommendations for future drilling based on problems we encountered the first time around, plus possible sites for a few more wells on the property." And that, she thought, should do it.

Big Jim handed the folders right back to her. Crossing his beefy arms in front of him, he settled on the edge of his desk. "I'm not here to fire you, Josie."

Watching her dainty mother settle gingerly on the

edge of the beat-up sofa, Josie flushed. "I can't imagine why not," she told her dad ruefully, "after the way I behaved."

Big Jim looked out the window at the drilling rig, then back to Josie. "You struck oil," he reminded her proudly.

Unable to sit still for one second since she and Wade had called it quits the night before, Josie paced back and forth.

"Yes, I struck oil," she reiterated wearily, wishing she could be even one-tenth as proud of herself as her father seemed to be this morning. "But only by using every trick in the book to usurp the authority to do so." Looking back, Josie still couldn't believe she had ever gotten so carried away with ambition.

"That's true," Big Jim agreed sagely, "but you're not going to do it again."

"You've got that right!" Josie sighed. She halted in front of the window. She saw Ernie, Gus and Dieter on the derrick platform, getting ready to meet with the production crew that would soon be arriving to make arrangements to pump the oil they'd found out of the ground.

"What you did took guts," Big Jim continued gently. When Josie said nothing in response, he got up, crossed to her side and put his hands on her shoulders. "I was wrong not to give you the same chance I would have given any son of mine, Josie," he told her gruffly.

Hardly able to believe what she was hearing, Josie turned to face him. "But I am prepared to rectify that now by doing what I should have done from the first," Big Jim continued seriously. "And that is welcome you into the company I started with open arms. I'm making you a vice president of Wyatt Drilling and putting you in charge of all operations here while I'm in South America for the next six months. You can hire more staff, run things the way you please and take the jobs you want. There's only one concession on your part, Josie, and it's one your mother and I absolutely insist on." Big Jim paused to look at Bitsy. "No more using your Corbett family trust fund to finance any further oil exploration. I'm giving you a Wyatt Drilling Company budget and you have to stick to it, come what may. Agreed?" he stipulated heavily.

"Agreed," Josie said, feeling both joy that she'd finally made her lifelong dream of being a lady wildcatter come true, and relief that she'd finally set things to right with her family.

If only the rest of her life could be as quickly and easily straightened out, she thought wistfully.

"You don't look very happy, darling," Bitsy noted gently, coming up to stand on the other side of Josie.

Josie basked in the comfort and understanding her parents were giving her. She paused, finally feeling secure enough in their love for her to be able to confide her innermost fears. "I just wish I felt better about how I got this," she said softly. She wished she felt better about the unconscionable way she had deceived and, yes, used Wade. Because the truth was, the end did not justify the means. Not ever. And if she had realized that earlier, she might not have found—and fallen head over heels in love with—and then finally lost Wade.

"Look, the way it happened aside," Big Jim told

Josie, leading her over to the sofa, "I'm very impressed by what you did here and so is your mother."

"Your father and I were up most of the night talking, Josie." Bitsy guided Josie to a seat in the middle of the sofa. She sat on one side of Josie. Big Jim the other. "He made me see you have a real talent for wildcatting," Bitsy continued. "And, as much as I'm loath to admit it, Josie, even I can see that you love this a lot more than you ever did working in an office at the foundation. So, no more pushing you to go back to Dallas," Bitsy said firmly. "It's a new world and time I joined it."

"There's only one thing left to be worked out," Big Jim said with a look at Bitsy.

Bitsy nodded in total agreement with her ex-husband. She leaned forward and clasped Josie's hand. "What about Wade?" Bitsy asked Josie with a gentle, understanding glance.

Finding she could no longer sit still, Josie surged from the sofa and began to pace once again. "It's too late for us," she told her parents grimly, wishing with all her heart that things were different, but suspecting sadly they never would be.

"Maybe not," Bitsy said gently.

Josie had kept hoping he'd come to his senses and come after her, forgive her and give her another chance. But that was unrealistic. She knew how he felt about loyalty and trust. She'd failed him on both counts. Like it or not, there was no chance in all of Texas that he'd forgive her for that.

"You're a fool if you let this one get away."

Wade looked up to see all three of his brothers striding into his ranch house. Scowling at them all, he went back to packing up his belongings.

Shane lounged in the doorway. He curved both his hands around his National Rodeo Champion belt buckle. "I told you we didn't have a minute to spare," he said to Jackson and Travis.

Wade scowled. He was in no mood for company and probably wouldn't be for some time. "Spare me the man-to-man speeches, guys." He didn't need his three brothers telling him how swiftly Josie had turned his entire life upside down, or that she had changed him in ways that no one had thought possible.

For the first time in his life, he felt that there were other things beside the bottom line, besides dollars and cents. She had made him feel as if he did have a heart. And knew exactly what to do and say and how to get close to another human being. She had made him feel that he wouldn't have to spend the rest of his life alone, settling for inane small talk and meaningless affairs instead of heart-to-heart talks and soulful lovemaking.

When he had been with Josie, he had seen his future, had felt he could have everything he'd begun to fear was permanently out of his reach. Only to be duped again!

What was wrong with him that he hadn't seen this coming? Wade wondered furiously. That he could be so blindsided again? There were limits, after all, to how much and how often a man could be hurt and humiliated.

Jackson—who had apparently come straight from the hospital—was still in surgical scrubs. He rubbed his jaw and studied Wade thoughtfully. "It's never been that you don't have a heart or that you have a calculator and dollar signs in the place where your heart should be. It's just you don't know how to use it."

The hell he didn't, Wade thought, as he stuffed underwear and socks in his suitcase on top of his jeans. He had loved and trusted Josie. But she hadn't loved and trusted him. Wade reached for his freshly laundered shirts, ripped them off the hangers and stuffed them on top of the rest of his clothes. "From this point on I'm going to stick to what I know—business and hopelessly shallow women. No more women who seem sincere but aren't," he vowed resolutely. Slamming his suitcase shut, he headed for his laptop computer in the next room.

Exchanging concerned looks, his three brothers followed. "Look, we know Josie wasn't your usual type," Travis said, pushing the brim of his Stetson back and looking like the veteran cattle rancher he was. "But she brought a light to your eyes and a smile to your face that made every one of the rest of us McCabes do a double take."

"The fact Josie's really a debutante and an heiress in her own right shouldn't matter one whit," Shane added.

"Even though you did commit a major faux pas in making it known you were trying to turn her into a lady," Jackson observed as Wade began packing up his laptop computer.

"She didn't need or want lessons on that," Wade said, acutely aware all over again how he had made a fool of himself, and all in the name of love.

"Which maybe," Shane guessed quite accurately, "was what made it so much fun."

Unfortunately, that was the truth, too, Wade thought uncomfortably. He'd had tons of fun with Josie. Worse, the thought of a life without her was almost more than he could bear.

"Look," Shane continued determinedly, "I'm the last person in the world to tell anyone to get married. But in your case I'm gonna make an exception."

"We saw the two of you together last night. If ever there were two people who were meant to be together..." Jackson said.

Wade looked at Travis. "Et tu, Brutus?" he said lightly.

Travis—who'd hated to discuss anything the least bit romantic ever since he'd lost his own fiancée in a car accident—said, "She's the only woman who made you forget about business. She's got to be special." Travis paused, his face reflecting the hurt he had suffered and the hope he felt for Wade. "Special isn't easy to find. If I were you," he said softly, "I wouldn't turn my back on it and walk away."

Bitsy soaked two compresses in ice water. Bracelets jingling, she wrung the soft cotton squares out and handed them over to her daughter. "I'm glad you're going to the She's Marrying Him All Over Again bridal shower for Lilah McCabe tonight."

Josie refused to stay home and feel sorry for herself, or shed even one more tear!—so she figured she might as well go along to the big bash with her mother, who had also been invited by Lilah. Besides, everything in this trailer, everything on the Golden Slipper Ranch, reminded her of Wade. And she certainly needed to get away from that, now that they were no longer an item, Josie told herself.

Studying her red, puffy eyes in the mirror, Josie frowned. And forced herself to adapt a cheerful attitude. "It's supposed to rival the bachelor party they gave for John McCabe a couple of weeks ago."

"Wild, hmm?" Bitsy looked excited about the prospect of that.

"And then some." Josie dropped onto the rumpled covers of her bed. She stretched out, head on the pillows. She pressed the icy compresses against her eyes, to take down the last of the tear-induced swelling. "Jackson McCabe's new bride, Lacey, stripped down to a gold lamé bikini and danced on the bar that night. Of course they weren't married yet when it happened. In fact they hadn't even met. But once they did—and she lassoed him to a chair—there was no turning back for either of them. They were married in no time flat!"

"I'm sure they had their up-and-down moments, too," Bitsy said.

Josie's lips formed a testy pout. "But they got together in the end," Josie said. She and Wade hadn't and wouldn't, and for that she feared her heart would ache until her dying day.

Bitsy circled closer and perched on the edge of the bed. "Honey, if you love him as much as I think you do, maybe you should swallow your pride and just telephone Wade. I spoke to Lilah this morning and she and I both think—"

Josie sat up abruptly. She ripped the icy cold compresses from her eyes. "Mom, don't start. It's over, okay?" Josie vaulted from the bed, nearly tripping over the sack of clean laundry that she'd not yet had the time—or the inclination—to put away. Josie marched to the closet. She pulled out the only clothes that were suitable for the gala—a sexy scoop-necked light blue denim sundress that laced up the back. And a pair of matching light blue denim espadrilles.

Josie shucked off her robe and began to dress. "I have to go on with my life, and that is exactly what I am going to do," she said emphatically.

To Josie's immense relief, Bitsy seemed to sense it was better not to disagree. So, gathering up their presents for Lilah, they headed off for the party. The all-woman event was in full swing as they arrived at Remington's Bar & Grill. Loud music and the sound of feminine laughter spilled out onto the street. Josie plastered a big smile on her face, as though she hadn't a care in the world, and marched in, her mother at her side. Streamers, balloons, flowers and a big banner in the shape of wedding bells decorated the inside of the restaurant. All four Lockhart sisters were there. Jackson's new wife, Lacey. Plus Lacey's mom. And new Laramie resident Patricia Weatherby.

Lilah McCabe took Josie's arm. She led her toward the bar. "Let's get you some champagne, dear. Then I'll introduce you to the mayor's wife."

Josie was about to pick up her glass when there was a commotion at the door behind her. Wade McCabe marched in, John Wayne style. He was clad in tight-fitting black jeans, a white shirt, taupe sport coat, boots and Stetson. Ignoring the gasps and chuckles, he headed straight for Josie.

"I want to talk to you."

Pushing the memory of the passion they had shared from her mind, she turned away and headed for the bar. "It's too late for talking, Wade." He had broken her heart, walking away from her that way. Refusing to listen to her. To forgive. She wasn't going to give him a chance to stomp on her heart all over again.

Wade braced a hand on the bar beside her. "It's only too late if I say it is." He stepped closer, invading her space, his voice so quiet she had to strain to hear him.

Josie plucked a long-stemmed flute, brimming with bubbly golden liquid, from the bar. Keeping her eyes directed away from his sexy, compelling gaze, she raised it and took a sip for courage. Much more of this closeness and she'd end up in his arms. "Forget it, Wade. We have already said everything there is to say." She was finished with men who couldn't accept her as she was, flaws, idiosyncrasies, mistakes, and all.

Wade took up the challenge. Wordlessly he plucked the champagne flute from her hand and set it aside. Josie only had to look at his face to know the game plan—he was planning to swing her up in his arms and carry her out. But he wasn't going to succeed, she thought grimly, as she dashed around a table, putting it between them. "You are making a spectacle of us!" she said as he merrily gave chase.

"Like you made a spectacle out of me?" he asked in a low voice. The new determination in his voice had her pulse jumping.

"You're the one who pursued me!" Josie fumed, hot, embarrassed color flooding her cheeks.

"As I recall you let yourself get caught!" Wade drawled, his smile so wicked it made her heart race.

Josie glared at him even as she darted away. "My mistake!"

"No," Wade replied as he closed in on her with a purposefulness that had her trembling. "My mistake, the only mistake," he continued in a low seductive voice, "was in letting you walk away."

Hurriedly, she tried to edge past him, heading toward the door. Where she moved, he followed, easily blocking her moves. As they continued their dance, Josie's exasperation with him increased by leaps and bounds. She hadn't felt like this since she was in elementary school, being chased by the boys at recess.

"Stop chasing me this instant!" Josie fumed.

"Gladly!" Grinning mischievously, Wade closed the distance between them. Applause, hooting, and hollering erupted all around them as he caught her beneath the knees, lifted her off her feet and swept her gallantly up into his arms.

"Wade McCabe, you put me down this instant!" Josie ordered hotly as he cradled her tenderly against his chest. "I mean it! We are finished. You hear me?"

"Lady, we haven't even begun," Wade told her with a cheerful, determined smile.

He swept through the doors, heading straight for the stagecoach at the curb. Not surprisingly that, too, was a family affair. Shane McCabe was holding the door open. Travis McCabe was atop it, handling the reins. Big Jim, John McCabe and Jackson McCabe were all out on the curb, watching the spectacle and egging Wade on with grins and whistles. As if he needed any prodding, Josie fumed.

Josie glared at her father. "I can't believe this! You're encouraging him, too?"

Big Jim shrugged and grinned. He rubbed a hand across his jaw. "Given the way you respond to him?" Big Jim drawled as people from the party streamed into the street. "Yeah, I think Wade ought to give it another shot." Big Jim shook his index finger at her. "You should, too, honey," he finished gently.

"I'll second that!" John McCabe said. "We all think you'd be a fine addition to our family." His enthusiastic declaration of support was followed by more hooting and hollering.

Wade lifted Josie into the coach, where flowers and a bottle of champagne awaited. He set her on the seat, then followed her inside. The door clicked behind them. Wade lifted his fist to the ceiling and pounded on it twice. The coach took off to the accompaniment of much cheering and shouted encouragement.

Hardly able to believe this was happening to her, Josie settled back onto the seat. She decided it was undignified to struggle anymore. She would just listen to what he had to say, tell him they were still through and let that be that. "Where did this—this coach—come from?" Josie demanded irritably. Honestly! She wouldn't have gotten all gussied up, had she known he was going to spirit her away to parts unknown in a stagecoach!

Wade tipped the brim of his hat back and settled on the opposite seat. "The town uses it for their annual Old West Days festival at the end of July. I talked the mayor into letting me use it for the evening so I could make your Cinderella dreams come true."

At that, Josie didn't know whether to laugh or cry. She was touched at the amount of trouble he had gone to. "Where are you taking me?" she demanded, as the stagecoach rolled along the smoothly paved streets of Laramie, toward the outskirts of town.

Wade winked. "That's for me to know and you to find out."

"Like heck it is!" Josie raised a fist to the ceiling of the coach, intending to signal them to stop. Wade caught her hand and tugged her close. They collided, softness to hardness. He hooked his other arm around her waist, tugged her down onto his lap and guided her between his spread knees, all in one smooth motion.

"I still want to know where we're going!" Josie said. Determined not to give in to him, she folded her arms in front of her.

He looked down at her hotly and teased, "Nowhere the least bit frilly and ladylike, that's for sure."

Josie continued to glower at him, and she did not uncross her arms, even when he tried to pry them lose. "What for?" She pulled her upper body as far away from him as he would allow. "To prove I don't matter to you?"

Wade shook his head. "To prove I accept you, just the way you are, mistakes and all. See, the truth is," Wade rushed on as he tightened his possessive grip on her waist, "I knew you weren't like Sandra. With Sandra, we were so out of tune that even after two years of dating I hadn't a clue she was unhappy. But with you, Josie," Wade continued softly, his brown eyes roving her face, "I saw the signs. There were at least a dozen times this past week, whenever the subject of Big Jim or your life in Dallas came up, when I knew—" he pointed to his heart and his head "—in here and in here, that you were uncomfortable, maybe even hiding something." Wade drew a deep breath. His voice dropped another notch. "I also knew what you were doing when you distracted me from reading the day's news on the Internet. Just like I knew that when we kissed and made love it had been because you were as caught up in the passion and feeling as I was.

"And I got to thinking," he continued, taking his hat off and putting it on the seat beside him, "if we were that in sync with each other after just a few days, what would it be like after a month, a year, a decade of togetherness? The bottom line is I love you, Josie. I love you with all my heart and soul."

"Oh, Wade," Josie whispered thickly as tears of happiness welled up in her eyes, "I love you, too." She hugged him fiercely. "So much."

"Then marry me," Wade urged hoarsely.

Josie wanted to. So much. But before she could take such a giant step there were things that she needed to lay on the line. Things she needed him to know. "I'm not giving up my career," she cautioned. Her success had been too hard won.

Wade lifted her hand to his lips and kissed it gently. "I don't want you to."

Her hand tingling from the sensual kiss, Josie swallowed. "I'm not ever going to be a society belle, either."

Wade smiled, the contentment he felt at just being with her like this again obvious. "I've had enough glitter to last me a lifetime," he told her solemnly.

Josie ran her fingers through the windswept layers

of his ash brown hair and looked into his eyes. "What I am willing to be is a businesswoman, a wildcatter, wife and mother all in one."

Wade grinned at her in a way that let her know she was exactly what he wanted in a wife and always would be. "And in return I promise you I'll be the best husband, lover, life partner and father of your children you could ever want." He drew her to him for a long, sexy kiss. "So what do you think? Four or five kids sound about right to you?"

Josie smiled as she envisioned the two of them living together as man and wife and sharing the parenting of a big, happy brood. "Sounds perfect," she said softly.

"Then I better get a ring on your finger, hadn't I," Wade teased, drawing her close for another long and tender kiss, "so we can get started making all our dreams come true."

"You've got a plan for that, too?" Josie teased. She nestled against him contentedly.

Mischief sparkling in his eyes, Wade looked at her in a way that said he still had a few surprises up his sleeve. He thumped on the ceiling of the stagecoach twice, signaling his brothers.

"Oh, yeah," he promised softly, "I do."

* * * * *